Oliver Twist

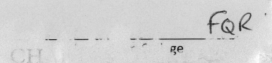

FQR

ge

Level 6

Retold by Latif Doss

Series Editors: Andy Hopkins and Jocelyn Potter

Pearson Education Limited
Edinburgh Gate, Harlow,
Essex CM20 2JE, England
and Associated Companies throughout the world.

ISBN: 978-1-4058-6525-8

First published in the Bridge Series 1962
This adaptation first published in the Longman Fiction Series 1996
First Penguin Books edition published 1999
This edition first published 2008

12

Text copyright © Penguin Books Ltd 1999
This edition copyright © Pearson Education Ltd 2008

Typeset by Graphicraft Ltd, Hong Kong
Set in 11/14pt Bembo
Printed in China
SWTC/12

Published by Pearson Education Ltd in association with
Penguin Books Ltd, both companies being subsidiaries of Pearson Plc

For a complete list of the titles available in the Penguin Readers series please write to your local
Pearson Longman office or to: Penguin Readers Marketing Department, Pearson Education,
Edinburgh Gate, Harlow, Essex CM20 2JE, England.

Contents

Introduction

He rose from the table and, advancing to the master, bowl in hand, said,
'Please, sir, I want some more.'

The master was a fat, healthy man, but he turned very pale. He stared
with horror and amazement at the small boy for some seconds.

'What!' he said finally in a faint voice.

'Please, sir,' replied Oliver, 'I want some more.'

Charles Dickens's delightful description of the poor, half-starved, nine-year-old Oliver Twist shocking the fat, healthy workhouse master by asking for more made his thousands of readers in mid-nineteenth century Britain laugh and cry. The scene has been repeated on the stage, in films, and in television dramas countless times, and the little orphan Oliver with his empty bowl has become a part of British national culture.

The story of Oliver Twist had already been filmed six times before the most famous version was made in 1948, directed by David Lean. A stage musical by Lionel Bart, based on the story and called *Oliver!*, full of humour, dance and delightful songs, was a great success in the 1960s and is still regularly performed. The film version, made in 1968, was an even greater success.

But there was a serious purpose to Dickens's original novel. He wanted to show his readers the terrible conditions in the state workhouses of that time, where the poor and the sick were forced to live; and in particular to show the cruelty, beatings and starvation of orphan children there. Charles Dickens was a new writer of fiction; this was his first real attempt at a novel, and the first written under his own name. But from his own difficult early life and his work as a journalist he had experience of the horrors of poverty.

Charles Dickens became one of the most popular writers of all time, creating some of the best-known characters in English literature. He was born in Portsmouth, an important port on the south coast of England, in 1812. His father was a clerk in the Navy Pay Office and for most of Charles's first ten years the family lived happily in Chatham, another naval town in Kent. His mother encouraged him to read from an early age, and he was a good pupil at a local school.

Unfortunately, his father was not a good manager of money and the family became poorer and poorer. When Charles was only ten years old, the family moved to a poor area of London. Two years later, they were deeply in debt. Charles's father was arrested and sent to prison, and Charles had to leave school and start to work. For six months he worked in a factory, doing hard and dirty work for little pay.

But during those first two years in London, he walked the streets and became familiar with all the areas of that great city and with its people, rich and poor. He also continued his reading and, after leaving school, began to work in lawyers' offices. He also started to write articles for newspapers and magazines about London and Londoners, using the name 'Boz'. By the age of twenty he was a reporter in the law courts and in Parliament. When he was twenty-four, his first collection of short pieces was published in book form as *Sketches by Boz*, and this was so popular that two other collections were published later.

At twenty-five he became editor of *Bentley's Miscellany*, a monthly magazine, and began to write chapters for it of a story called *The Parish Boy's Progress*. Under the pen-name 'Boz', he was at the same time regularly writing short, amusing stories about Mr Pickwick and his friends for another magazine, and these were becoming enormously popular. He continued to write these *Pickwick Papers* until 1837. He seemed to enjoy the pressure of work at this time, writing new stories about Pickwick, new chapters of *The Parish Boy's Progress* (later to be called *Oliver Twist*) as well as being both the editor and a writer of other pieces for his magazine. He wrote by hand, of course, and at great speed. His plots are often criticized for being loose and full of chance relationships and meetings. This cannot be denied, but the great strength of his writing was in his characters, and in the descriptions of real people and places based on his years as a journalist.

The success of *Oliver Twist* confirmed both his reputation and a large regular income, and he went on to write about twenty novels, most of which were published in monthly parts in magazines. He also wrote many short stories and articles, and works of non-fiction.

In his later novels, including *Hard Times*, *Little Dorrit* and *Our Mutual Friend*, he presents an even darker view of the world. His humour concentrates on the evil side of human experience, in particular the inhuman social consequences of the law, industry and trade.

A man of great energy, Dickens also found the time to work for a number of organizations that helped the poor and improved social conditions. In 1841 he travelled to the US, where he spoke against slavery, for which he was severely criticized by much of the American press.

His private life was not always happy. He married Catherine Hogarth in 1836 and they had ten children, but they separated in 1858. By then Dickens had fallen in love with a clever and charming young actress called Ellen Ternan. They met when she was eighteen and Dickens was forty-five. They continued a close relationship for the rest of Dickens's life, although it was kept a secret, as the public would have been very shocked to know of it.

Towards the end of his life, Dickens almost gave up writing and began to give dramatic readings of parts of his books to enthusiastic audiences. He greatly enjoyed doing this; it was exciting and theatrical. One of his favourite pieces was the murder of Nancy from *Oliver Twist*. He knew how this reading would affect his audience, and was delighted when ladies often fainted during the performance. The strain of these frequent readings, however, greatly raised his blood pressure, and without doubt contributed to his failing health at that time.

Dickens died in 1870, and there was great public grief at his death. After a big public funeral service he was buried in Westminster Abbey in London.

Oliver Twist was begun at a time when Dickens was both successful and extremely busy. The opening chapters were fairly simple and based to some extent on his own experiences as a child. He had just become a father for the first time and he knew how different his own child's life would be from the life of a poor, lonely orphan.

In 1834 a new Poor Law had been introduced by Parliament. It was an attempt to organize official workhouses for people who were poor, ill, old, or otherwise unable to work or look after themselves. These workhouses were run by groups of local people, usually wealthy and middle class. Life in these workhouses was deliberately made hard; husbands and wives were separated, and the food was very poor. The idea was to discourage idleness among people who were able to work. But the sick, the old and, especially, young children suffered badly.

Oliver is born in a workhouse; he is an orphan from the day of his birth. He is brought up without love or care, given the minimum of food and regularly beaten. At nine years old, he goes to a larger workhouse where he and other orphans exist under extreme conditions. Punished for showing some spirit, he is sold into employment with a coffin maker, where he continues to be treated very badly. For the first ten years of his life, he has no family, friends, care or love of any kind.

At last he runs away to London, arriving starved and exhausted, and is taken in by a gang of thieves who train him to steal. It is here that the mood of the book suddenly changes, as Dickens introduces his gang of villains: Fagin, the leader and teacher of the boys; the Artful Dodger and Charley Bates, his most skilful pupils; the murderously evil Bill Sikes. Dickens wrote about these criminals and their environment with enthusiasm and in great detail. At once there were protests from his readers. They did not want to read of such horrors. Dickens replied that he described these people as they really were, living in the dirtiest and poorest districts of London, running like rats from place to place, hiding from the police, and always facing the very real threat of hanging; hanging was the punishment for many crimes at that time. Dickens's description of London's criminals and how they existed opened the eyes of many of the 'better' people of London, who had little idea of where and how such people lived. Above all, Dickens made his criminals real villains, and in the end they got the punishment they deserved.

It must be remembered that London at this time was a mostly lawless place. Whole areas were occupied by criminals, and respectable people went into them at great risk. Pickpockets, burglars, thieves of all kinds were everywhere; physical attacks, even murders, were common for the theft of a purse. In 1829, Sir Robert (Bobby) Peel had created the first police force in the city in an attempt to control this growing crime wave. But his small band of policemen – 'Peelers', as they were called, and also later 'Bobbies' – were actually unpopular with ordinary people and received little help from them.

Many characters in *Oliver Twist* are either all goodness, like Rose Maylie and Mr Brownlow, or totally evil, like Fagin and Bill Sikes. Others are foolish, greedy and weak, even funny. And among them all goes little Oliver, holding the various parts of the story together. He suffers beatings, arrest, illness and shooting, but he remains an innocent to the end, astonished when he realizes that his companions are thieves, grateful for any signs of love and affection, and stirring motherly and sympathetic feelings even in the heart of a tough street woman like Bill Sikes's girlfriend, Nancy.

Chapter 1   Oliver Twist Is Born

Oliver Twist was born in a workhouse, and for a long time after his birth there was considerable doubt whether the child would live. He lay breathless for some time, trying to decide between this world and the next. After a few struggles, however, he breathed, coughed and gave a loud cry.

The pale face of a young woman was raised weakly from the bed, and in a faint voice she said, 'Let me see the child and die.'

'Oh, you must not talk about dying yet,' said the doctor, as he rose from where he was sitting near the fire and advanced towards her.

'Goodness, no!' added the poor old woman who was acting as nurse.

The doctor placed the child in its mother's arms; she pressed her cold white lips on its forehead; passed her hands over her face; looked wildly around, fell back – and died.

'It's all over,' said the doctor at last.

'Ah, poor dear, so it is!' said the old nurse.

'She was a good-looking girl, too,' added the doctor. 'Where did she come from?'

'She was brought here last night,' replied the old woman. 'She was found lying in the street. She had walked some distance, for her shoes were torn to pieces; but where she came from, or where she was going, nobody knows.'

'The old story,' said the doctor, shaking his head as he raised the dead woman's left hand. 'No wedding ring, I see. Ah! Good night!'

While the nurse dressed him, Oliver cried loudly. If he had known, though, what the future held for him, the motherless child would have cried even louder.

Chapter 2   Early Years

For the next eight or ten months Oliver was bottle-fed when anyone remembered to attend to him. Then he was sent to a smaller workhouse some three miles away, where twenty or thirty other young orphans rolled about the floor all day, without the inconvenience of too much food or too much clothing. They were in the charge of an elderly woman called Mrs Mann, who received from the government seven and a half pence each week for each child. Being a woman of wisdom and experience, she knew what was good for the children and what was good for herself. So she kept the greater part of the weekly allowance for her own use, and gave the children hardly enough to keep them alive.

It cannot be expected that this system of bringing up children would produce any very strong or healthy specimens. On his ninth birthday, Oliver Twist was a pale, weak child, very thin and rather below average height. But the child was full of spirit.

He was spending his ninth birthday in the coal cellar with two other children; they had, all three, been beaten by Mrs Mann and then locked up for daring to say they were hungry. Suddenly, Mrs Mann was surprised by the appearance of Mr Bumble, a workhouse official; a fat man, full of a sense of his own importance. The purpose of his visit was to take Oliver back to the large workhouse, for he was now too old to remain with Mrs Mann.

Oliver, whose face and hands had by this time been washed in a hurry, was led into the room by his kind-hearted protectress.

'Make a bow to the gentleman, Oliver,' said Mrs Mann.

Oliver obeyed.

'Will you go along with me, Oliver?' said Mr Bumble in his clear, ringing tones.

Oliver was about to say that he would be happy to go along

with anybody when, looking upward, he caught sight of Mrs Mann, who was standing behind Mr Dumble's chair and making threatening gestures at him. He understood what she meant at once.

'Will *she* go with me?' asked poor Oliver.

'No, she can't,' replied Mr Bumble. 'But she'll come and see you sometimes.'

Oliver pretended to be very sad at going away; it was easy for him to call tears into his eyes. Hunger and recent bad treatment are of great assistance if you want to cry; and Oliver cried very naturally indeed. Mrs Mann gave him a thousand kisses and, what Oliver wanted a great deal more, a piece of bread and butter, so that he should not seem too hungry when he got to the workhouse.

Oliver was led away by Mr Bumble from the home where not a single kind word or look had ever lighted the darkness of his early years.

♦

Life in the workhouse was very severe indeed. The members of the board of management had ruled that the children should work to earn their living, and that they should be given three meals of thin soup a day, with an onion twice a week and half a cake on Sundays.

The room in which the boys were fed was a large stone hall, with a huge pot at one end. Out of this the master, assisted by one or two women, served out the soup at mealtimes. Each boy had one small bowl, and nothing more – except on public holidays, when he had a small piece of bread as well. The bowls never needed washing. The boys polished them with their spoons till they shone again, and when they had performed this operation they would sit staring eagerly at the huge pot, as if they could have eaten that too.

Oliver Twist and his companions suffered terrible hunger in silence for three months; in the end they became so desperate that one boy, who was tall for his age, told the others that unless he had another bowl of soup every day, he was afraid he might some night eat the boy who slept next to him. He had a wild hungry eye, and they fully believed him. A council was held; votes were cast, and it fell to Oliver Twist to walk up to the master after supper that evening and ask for more.

The evening arrived; the boys took their places. The master, in his cook's uniform, stood beside the huge pot with his two assistants behind him; the soup was served out. It quickly disappeared; the boys whispered to each other and made signs to Oliver. He rose from the table and, advancing to the master, bowl in hand, said, 'Please, sir, I want some more.'

The master was a fat, healthy man, but he turned very pale. He stared with horror and amazement at the small boy for some seconds.

'What!' he said finally in a faint voice.

'Please, sir,' replied Oliver, 'I want some more.'

The master aimed a blow at Oliver's head with his big spoon; seized him tightly in his arms, and shouted for Mr Bumble.

Mr Bumble, hearing the cry and learning the cause of it, rushed into the room where members of the board were meeting and, addressing the gentleman at the head of the table, said: 'Mr Limbkins, I beg your pardon, sir. Oliver Twist has asked for more.'

There was general alarm. Horror showed on every face.

'For *more*!' said Mr Limbkins. 'Be calm, Bumble, and answer me clearly. Do you mean to say that he asked for more, after he had eaten the supper given by the board?'

'He did, sir,' replied Bumble.

'That boy will be hanged,' said one of the gentlemen on the board. 'I know that boy will be hanged one day.'

Oliver was locked up at once. Next morning a notice was put

up on the outside of the gate, offering a reward of five pounds to anybody who would take Oliver Twist away from the workhouse.

Chapter 3　A Chimney Sweep Offers to Take Oliver

For weeks after committing the crime of asking for more, Oliver remained a prisoner in the dark and lonely room to which he had been sent by the board as a punishment. But let it not be supposed by the enemies of 'the system' that Oliver, while a prisoner, was denied the benefit of exercise or the pleasure of society. As for exercise, it was nice cold weather, and he was allowed to wash himself every morning under the pump in a stone yard in the presence of Mr Bumble, who prevented his catching cold by the repeated use of a stick. As for society, he was carried every other day into the hall where the boys dined, and there he was publicly beaten as a warning and example.

It happened one morning that Mr Gamfield, a chimney sweep, was on his way down the High Street, wondering how to pay the rent he owed to his landlord. Passing the workhouse, his eyes fell on the notice on the gate. He walked closer to read it.

One of the gentlemen on the board was standing at the gate. The chimney sweep, observing him, told him that he wanted an apprentice and was ready to take the boy offered. The gentleman ordered him to walk in and took him to Mr Limbkins.

Arrangements were made. Mr Bumble was at once instructed that Oliver Twist and the papers for his apprenticeship were to be taken before the magistrate for approval that very afternoon.

On his way to the magistrate, Mr Bumble instructed Oliver that all he would have to do would be to look very happy and say, when the gentleman asked him if he wanted to be apprenticed, that he would like it very much indeed.

Eventually they arrived at the office and appeared before the magistrate, an old gentleman with a pair of eye-glasses.

'This is the boy, sir,' said Mr Bumble. 'Bow to the magistrate, my dear.'

Oliver made his best bow.

'Well,' said the old gentleman. 'I suppose he's fond of sweeping chimneys?'

'He's very fond of it, sir,' replied Bumble, giving Oliver a threatening look.

'And this man that's to be his master – you, sir – you'll treat him well, and feed him, and do all that sort of thing, will you?' said the old gentleman.

'When I say I will, I mean I will,' replied Mr Gamfield roughly.

'You're a rough speaker, my friend, but you look an honest, open-hearted man,' said the old gentleman, turning his eye-glasses in the direction of Gamfield, on whose face cruelty was clearly stamped. But the magistrate was half blind, so he could not reasonably be expected to see what other people saw.

The magistrate fixed his eye-glasses more firmly on his nose, and began to look about him for the inkpot.

It was a critical moment in Oliver's future. If the inkpot had been where the old gentleman thought it was, he would have been led away at once. But as it happened to be immediately under his nose, he looked all over his desk for it without finding it; and chancing in the course of his search to look straight ahead of him, his eyes met the pale and frightened face of Oliver Twist, who was staring at the cruel face of his future master with a mixture of horror and fear.

The old gentleman stopped, laid down his pen, and looked from Oliver to Mr Bumble.

'My boy!' said the old gentleman, leaning over the desk, 'you look pale and alarmed. What is the matter? Stand a little way from him, Mr Bumble. Now, boy, tell us what's the matter: don't be afraid.'

Oliver fell on his knees and, joining his hands together, begged the magistrate to order him back to the dark room – beat him – kill him if he liked – rather than send him away with that awful man.

'Well!' said Mr Bumble, raising his hands and eyes. 'Well! Of all the ungrateful orphans that I have ever seen, you are one of the most shameless.'

'Hold your tongue,' said the magistrate. 'I refuse to sign these papers.' He pushed the documents aside as he spoke. 'Take the boy back to the workhouse, and treat him kindly. He seems to need it.'

Next morning the public were again informed that five pounds would be paid to anybody who would take possession of Oliver Twist.

Chapter 4   Oliver Is Apprenticed to an Undertaker

Mr Bumble was returning one day to the workhouse when he met at the gate Mr Sowerberry, the undertaker, a tall, bony man dressed in a worn-out black suit. As Mr Sowerberry advanced to Mr Bumble, he shook him by the hand and said: 'I have taken the measurements of the two women that died last night, Mr Bumble.'

'You'll make your fortune, Mr Sowerberry,' said Mr Bumble.

'I think so,' said the undertaker. 'The prices allowed by the board are very small, Mr Bumble.'

'So are the coffins,' replied the latter.

Mr Sowerberry laughed for a long time at this joke. 'Well, well, Mr Bumble,' he said finally, 'I don't deny that, since the new system of feeding has been introduced, the coffins are somewhat narrower than they used to be; but we must have some profit, Mr Bumble. Wood is expensive, sir.'

'Well, well,' said Mr Bumble, 'every trade has its disadvantages.

By the way, you don't know anybody who wants a boy, do you?'

'Ah!' exclaimed the undertaker, 'that's the very thing I wanted to speak to you about. You know, Mr Bumble, I think I'll take the boy myself.'

Mr Bumble seized the undertaker by the arm and led him into the building, where it was quickly arranged that Oliver should go to him that evening.

Oliver heard this news in perfect silence and, carrying a brown-paper parcel in his hand, which was all the luggage he had, he was led away by Mr Bumble to a new scene of suffering.

For some time they walked in silence. As they drew near to Mr Sowerberry's shop, Mr Bumble looked down to make sure that the boy was clean and neat enough to be seen by his new master.

'Oliver!' said Mr Bumble. 'Pull that cap up off your eyes, and hold up your head.'

Oliver did as he was told at once, but when he looked up at Mr Bumble there were tears in his eyes. Mr Bumble stared at him coldly. The child made a brave attempt to stop crying, but the tears rolled down his cheeks and he covered his face with both hands.

'Well!' exclaimed Mr Bumble, stopping short and looking at him with hatred, 'of all the ungrateful and unpleasant boys I have ever seen, Oliver, you are the –'

'No, no, sir,' cried Oliver, holding tightly to the hand which held the stick; 'no, no, sir; I will be good indeed; indeed I will, sir! I am a very little boy, sir; and it is so – so . . .'

'So what?' inquired Mr Bumble in surprise.

'So lonely, sir! So very lonely!' cried the child.

The undertaker had just closed his shop and was writing the details of the day's business by lamplight when Mr Bumble entered.

'Here, Mr Sowerberry, I've brought the boy.'

'Oh! That's the boy, is it?' said the undertaker, raising the lamp above his head to get a better view of Oliver. 'Mrs Sowerberry, will you have the goodness to come here a moment, my dear?'

Mrs Sowerberry, a short, thin, bad-tempered woman, came in from a little room behind the shop.

'My dear,' said Mr Sowerberry, respectfully, 'this is the boy from the workhouse that I told you about.'

'Dear me!' she said. 'He's very small.'

'Yes, he is rather small,' replied Mr Bumble, 'but he'll grow, Mrs Sowerberry – he'll grow.'

'Ah! I dare say he will,' replied the lady angrily, 'on our food and drink. I see no use for workhouse children, not I; for they always cost more to keep than they are worth. However, men always think they know best. There! Get downstairs, little bag of bones.'

The undertaker's wife opened a side door and pushed Oliver down some stairs into a dark room which was used as a kitchen. In it sat an untidy girl in worn-out shoes and a torn blue dress.

'Here, Charlotte,' said Mrs Sowerberry, who had followed Oliver down, 'give this boy some of the cold bits of meat that were put aside for the dog. The dog hasn't come home since the morning, so he can go without them.'

Oliver's eyes shone at the mention of meat. A plateful of broken pieces was set before him, and he ate rapidly while Mrs Sowerberry watched him with silent horror. When he had finished, she ordered him to follow her and, taking a dirty lamp in one hand, she led the way upstairs again.

'Your bed is under the counter. You don't mind sleeping among the coffins, I suppose? But it doesn't matter whether you do or don't, for you can't sleep anywhere else.'

Oliver obediently followed her.

послушно

Chapter 5   Noah Claypole

Oliver, being left to himself in the undertaker's shop, set the lamp down on a bench and looked around him. An unfinished coffin which stood in the middle of the shop made him tremble with fear every time his eyes wandered in its direction; he almost expected to see some terrible form raise its head out of it to drive him mad with terror.

He was woken in the morning by a loud kicking at the outside of the shop door and he hurried to unlock the chain.

'Open the door, will you?' an angry voice kept saying, while he did this.

'It will be open soon, sir,' replied Oliver, turning the key and removing the chain.

'I suppose you're the new boy, are you?' said the voice.

'Yes, sir,' replied Oliver.

'How old are you?' inquired the voice.

'Ten, sir,' replied Oliver.

'Then I'll whip you when I get in,' said the voice and, having made this kind promise, the speaker began to whistle.

Oliver pulled back the bolts with a trembling hand, and opened the door. He looked up the street and down the street, but he saw nobody but a slightly older boy, sitting on a post in front of the house and eating bread and butter.

'I beg your pardon, sir,' said Oliver finally, seeing that no other visitor made his appearance, 'did you knock?'

'I kicked,' replied the boy.

'Did you want a coffin, sir?' asked Oliver. At this the older boy looked cross and said that Oliver would soon want one himself if he continued to make jokes with his seniors.

'You don't know who I am, I suppose, Workhouse?' said the boy.

'No, sir,' replied Oliver.

'I'm Mr Noah Claypole,' said the boy. 'And you work under me.' With this, Mr Claypole gave Oliver a kick and entered the shop.

Mr and Mrs Sowerberry came down soon after that and Oliver followed Noah downstairs.

'Come near the fire, Noah,' said Charlotte. 'I saved a nice bit of bacon for you from the master's breakfast. Oliver, shut that door behind Mr Noah, and take your tea to that box and drink it there. Do you hear?'

'Do you hear, Workhouse?' said Noah Claypole.

Charlotte burst out laughing and Noah joined in. Then they both looked contemptuously at poor Oliver Twist as he sat trembling on the box in the coldest corner of the room, and ate the broken pieces which had been specially reserved for him.

Noah was a charity-boy, but not an orphan; he lived at home but was supported by public money because his mother was a poor washerwoman and his father a drunken, out-of-work soldier. For several months Oliver suffered Noah's ill-treatment of him without complaint, until one day something happened which indirectly produced a change in Oliver's life.

Oliver and Noah had gone down into the kitchen at the usual dinner hour. Noah put his feet on the tablecloth and pulled Oliver's hair in order to annoy him. Since Oliver did not cry, he said to him: 'Workhouse! How's your mother?'

'She's dead,' replied Oliver. 'Don't say anything about her to me!'

Oliver reddened as he said this; he breathed quickly, and there was a strange movement of the mouth and nose which Mr Claypole thought must be signs of an approaching fit of crying. He therefore returned to his insulting words.

'What did she die of, Workhouse?' he said.

'Of a broken heart, an old nurse told me,' replied Oliver, as a tear rolled down his cheek.

'What has made you cry now?'

'Not you,' replied Oliver, quickly brushing the tear away. 'Don't imagine it's you.'

'Oh, not me, eh!' said Noah.

'No, not you,' replied Oliver, sharply. 'There, that's enough. You'd better not say anything more to me about her!'

'Better not!' exclaimed Noah. 'Well! Better not! Workhouse, don't be rude. You know, Workhouse, your mother was a bad woman.'

'What did you say?' inquired Oliver, coldly.

'A bad woman, Workhouse,' replied Noah. 'And it's a good thing she died when she did, or else she would have been doing hard labour in prison, or she might have been hanged, which is more likely.'

Red with anger, Oliver jumped to his feet; seized Noah by the throat; shook him hard, and knocked him to the ground.

'He'll murder me!' shouted Noah. 'Charlotte! The new boy is going to murder me! Help! Help! Charlotte! Mrs Sowerberry! Help!'

Noah's shouts were answered by a loud scream from Charlotte, and a louder one from Mrs Sowerberry, and they both rushed into the kitchen.

'*Oh*, you little horror!' screamed Charlotte, seizing Oliver with all her strength, and giving him several blows.

Then Mrs Sowerberry joined in. She held Oliver with one hand, and ran the sharp nails on her other hand across his face. Now the danger had passed, Noah rose from the ground and beat him with a stick from behind. When they were all tired out, they dragged Oliver, struggling and shouting, into the cellar, and there locked him up. When this was done, Mrs Sowerberry sank into a chair and burst into tears.

'Dear, dear, she's going to faint!' said Charlotte. 'A glass of water, Noah, please. Quickly!'

'Oh! Charlotte,' said Mrs Sowerberry, almost unable to breathe from the cold water which Noah had poured over her head and shoulders. 'We are fortunate that we have not all been murdered in our beds!'

'Fortunate indeed, madam,' was the reply. 'I only hope this will teach master not to take in any more of these terrible creatures that are born to be murderers and robbers. Poor Noah! He was near death, madam, when I came in.'

'Poor fellow!' said Mrs Sowerberry, looking sympathetically at the boy. 'What shall we do? Your master's not at home; there's not a man in the house, and he'll kick that door down in ten minutes.'

'Dear, dear. I don't know, madam,' said Charlotte, 'unless we send for the police officers.'

'No, no,' said Mrs Sowerberry. 'Run to Mr Bumble, Noah, and tell him to come here directly. Never mind your cap; go quickly!'

Noah ran as fast as he could until he reached the workhouse gate. Having rested here for a minute or so, to collect some nice large tears, he knocked loudly at the gate.

'Mr Bumble! Mr Bumble!' cried Noah so loudly that Mr Bumble, who happened to be nearby, was alarmed and rushed into the yard without his hat.

'Oh, Mr Bumble, sir!' said Noah. 'Oliver, sir – Oliver has . . .'

'What? What?' interrupted Mr Bumble. 'Not run away; he hasn't run away, has he, Noah?'

'No, sir, no. Not run away, sir, but he's turned wild,' replied Noah. 'He tried to murder me, sir, and then tried to murder Charlotte, and then Mrs Sowerberry. Oh! What a pain he has caused me, sir!' And here Noah twisted his body like a snake, thus giving Mr Bumble the impression that he was badly hurt.

Mr Bumble, putting on his hat and taking his stick, accompanied Noah Claypole with all speed to the undertaker's shop.

Mr Sowerberry had not returned, and Oliver continued to kick at the cellar door. Mr Bumble returned the kicks from the outside and then, applying his mouth to the keyhole, said in a deep, impressive tone: 'Oliver!'

'Let me out!' replied Oliver from the inside.

'Do you know this voice, Oliver?' said Mr Bumble.

'Yes,' replied Oliver.

'Aren't you afraid of it, sir? Aren't you trembling while I speak, sir?' demanded Mr Bumble.

'No!' replied Oliver confidently.

Mr Bumble stepped back from the keyhole, drew himself up to his full height, and looked from one to another of those who were watching.

'Oh, you know, Mr Bumble, he must be mad,' said Mrs Sowerberry. 'No boy in half his senses would dare to speak to you like that.'

'It's not madness, madam,' replied Mr Bumble, after a moment's thought. 'It's meat.'

'What?' exclaimed Mrs Sowerberry.

'Meat, madam, meat,' replied Mr Bumble. 'You've fed him too much, madam. If you had kept the boy on soup, madam, this would never have happened.'

'Dear, dear!' exclaimed Mrs Sowerberry. 'This is the result of being generous!'

'Ah!' said Mr Bumble. 'The only thing that can be done now is to leave him in the cellar for a day or so, till he's really hungry; and to take him out, and keep him on soup all through his apprenticeship. He comes from a bad family, Mrs Sowerberry! Both the nurse and the doctor said that his mother had made her way here despite difficulties and pain that would have killed any good woman weeks before.'

At this point in Mr Bumble's speech Oliver, just hearing enough to know that some new reference was being made to his mother, started kicking violently at the door again. At this moment Sowerberry returned. Oliver's offence having been explained to him in enough detail to make him shake with anger, he unlocked the cellar door and dragged Oliver out by the collar.

Oliver's clothes had been torn in the beating he had received, his face was bruised and bleeding, and his hair was scattered over his forehead. But the angry colour had not disappeared, and when he was pulled out of his prison he looked at Noah completely without fear.

'Now, you're a nice young fellow, aren't you?' said Sowerberry, giving Oliver a shake and hitting him across one ear.

'He called my mother names,' replied Oliver.

'Well, and what if he did, you ungrateful child?' said Mrs Sowerberry. 'She deserved what he said, and worse.'

'She didn't,' said Oliver.

'She did,' said Mrs Sowerberry.

'It's a lie,' said Oliver.

Mrs Sowerberry burst into a flood of tears.

This flood of tears left Mr Sowerberry no choice; so he at once gave Oliver a good beating which satisfied even Mrs Sowerberry herself and made Mr Bumble's use of his stick, which followed, rather unnecessary. For the rest of the day Oliver was shut up in the back kitchen and at night Mrs Sowerberry ordered him upstairs to his bed.

It was not until he was left alone in the silence of the undertaker's dark workshop that Oliver gave way to his feelings. He had listened to their insults with contempt, and he had suffered the beatings without a cry. But now, when there was nobody to see or hear him, he fell upon his knees on the floor and, hiding his face in his hands, he cried such tears, as, please God, few so young may ever have cause to pour out.

For a long time Oliver remained motionless in this position. The lamp was burning low when he rose to his feet. Having looked slowly around him, and listened carefully, he gently undid the bolts and chains on the door and glanced outside.

It was a cold, dark night. There was no wind, and the dark shadows thrown by the trees on the ground looked frightening. He closed the door again, tied up the few articles of clothing he had, and sat down on a bench to wait for morning.

With the first light that struggled through the windows, Oliver rose and again unlocked the door. After a brief pause in the doorway, he stepped outside, closed the door behind him and was in the open street.

Chapter 6   The Artful Dodger

By eight o'clock Oliver was nearly five miles away from the town, but he ran for a time and then hid for a while in case he was being pursued. Then he sat down to rest beside a milestone and began to think, for the first time, where he could go.

The milestone told him, in big letters, that he was now seventy miles from London. The name fixed in his mind and gave him a new idea. London! The big city! Nobody could ever find him there! He had often heard the old men in the workhouse, too, say that no lad with spirit would find it difficult to earn his living in London. As these thoughts passed through his mind, he jumped to his feet and continued walking.

Oliver walked twenty miles that day, and all that time tasted nothing but a piece of dry bread. When night came, he turned into a field, and soon fell asleep.

He felt cold and stiff when he got up the next morning, and so hungry that he had to spend the only penny he had on a small loaf. Another night passed in the cold air made him worse, and when he set out on his journey the next morning, he could hardly move.

He continued in this way for six days, begging at cottage doors in the villages where it was not forbidden to beg. Early on the seventh morning after he had left his home town, he walked slowly and painfully into a little place called Barnet. The streets were empty; not a soul had woken to begin the business of the day. The sun was rising in all its beauty, but the light only served to show the boy his loneliness as he sat, with bleeding feet and covered with dust, on a doorstep.

He had been sitting on the doorstep for some time when he noticed that a boy who had passed him some minutes before had returned and was now looking at him closely from the opposite side of the street. After a while the boy crossed over and, walking up close to Oliver, said: 'Hullo! What's the trouble?'

The boy who addressed Oliver in this manner was about his own age, but one of the strangest-looking boys Oliver had ever seen. He was a dirty little boy, but he appeared to have all the manners of a man. He was short for his age, with sharp, ugly little eyes. His hat was stuck on the top of his head so lightly that it threatened to fall off at any moment. He wore a man's coat, which reached nearly to his heels. He had turned the arms back so that he could put his hands in his trouser pockets. He was, all in all, as proud and confident a young gentleman as ever stood four feet six, or something less.

'I am very hungry and tired,' replied Oliver, with tears in his eyes as he spoke. 'I have walked a long way. I have been walking for seven days.'

'Walking for seven days!' said the young gentleman. 'You want some food, and you shall have it. I am a poor boy myself, but I have a coin or two and I'll pay. Get up and come with me.'

Helping Oliver to rise, this young man took him to a neighbouring shop, where he bought him some meat and a big loaf of bread. Then he took him to a small public house, where a pot of beer was brought to him.

'Going to London?' said the strange boy, when Oliver had finally finished his meal.

'Yes.'

'Got anywhere to stay?'

'No.'

'Money?'

'No.'

The strange boy whistled, and put his hands into his pockets as far as the long arms of his coat would let them go.

'Do you live in London?' inquired Oliver.

'Yes, I do, when I'm at home,' replied the boy. 'I suppose you want a bed for tonight, don't you?'

'I do indeed,' answered Oliver. 'I have not slept under a roof for more than a week.'

'Don't cry,' said the young gentleman. 'I've got to be in London tonight. I know a respectable old gentleman who lives there, and he'll give you a bed for nothing if any gentleman he knows introduces you. And he knows me very well.'

This unexpected offer of shelter was too attractive to resist; especially as it was immediately followed by the assurance that the old gentleman would provide Oliver with a comfortable job, without loss of time. This led to a more friendly conversation between the two boys, from which Oliver discovered that his friend's name was Jack Dawkins, but that among his close friends he was called 'The Artful Dodger'.

As Jack Dawkins objected to their entering London before nightfall, it was nearly eleven o'clock when they reached the edge of the city.

They passed through one of the ugliest and dirtiest parts of London until at last they reached the bottom of a hill. Oliver was just wondering whether or not to run away, when the Dodger pushed open the door of a house and, pulling him into the passage, closed it behind them.

He gave a whistle and a faint light shone on the wall at the end of the passage. This was followed slowly by a man's face.

'There's two of you,' said the man, shading his eyes with his hand. 'Who's the other one?'

'A new friend,' replied Jack Dawkins, pulling Oliver forward. 'Is Fagin upstairs?'

'Yes, he's sorting the handkerchiefs. Go on up!' First the light and then the face disappeared.

Oliver, feeling his way with one hand, and the other firmly held by his companion, climbed the dark and broken stairs with some difficulty. Jack Dawkins threw open the door of a back room and pulled Oliver in after him.

The walls and ceiling of the room were completely black with age and dirt. There was a wooden table in front of the fire, on which were a candle, stuck in a beer bottle, two or three cups, a loaf and butter, and a plate. In a pan on the fire some sausages were cooking; standing over them was a very old Jew, whose evil-looking face was partly hidden by his thick, red hair. He was dressed in a dirty woollen coat, and he seemed to be dividing his attention between the cooking pan and a number of silk handkerchiefs which were hanging on a line. Several rough beds made of old cloths were laid side by side on the floor. Seated round the table were four or five boys, none older than the Dodger, smoking long clay pipes and drinking spirits with the air of middle-aged men. These crowded round the Dodger as he whispered a few words to the old man and then turned round and looked at Oliver. The old man turned too.

'This is him, Fagin,' said the Dodger. 'My friend, Oliver Twist.'

The old man smiled and, making a low bow to Oliver, took him by the hand and hoped he would have the honour of his friendship. Upon this the young gentlemen with the pipes approached and shook both his hands very hard, especially the one in which he held his few clothes.

'We are very glad to see you, Oliver,' said the old man. 'Dodger, take off the sausages, and pull a chair near the fire for Oliver. Ah, you're looking at the handkerchiefs, eh, my dear? We've just sorted them out, ready for the wash; that's all, Oliver; that's all. Ha! ha! ha!'

The last part of his speech was greeted with a loud shout of laughter from all the pupils of the cheerful old gentleman, and then they all sat down again to eat supper.

Chapter 7   Fagin and his Band

It was late next morning when Oliver awoke. There was no other person in the room but the old man, who was making himself some coffee for breakfast and whistling softly to himself.

Although Oliver was conscious of the old man's movements, he was still in a state of semi-consciousness between sleeping and waking. When the coffee was ready, the old man stood for a few minutes as if he did not know what to do next; then he turned round and looked at Oliver and called him by his name. He did not answer and certainly appeared to be asleep. The old man now stepped gently to the door and locked it. He then pulled out from some secret hole in the floor a small box, which he placed carefully on the table. His eyes shone as he raised the lid and looked in. Dragging an old chair to the table, he sat down and took out of the box an expensive-looking gold watch, shining with jewels.

'Ah!' said Fagin to himself with an ugly, twisted smile. 'Clever dogs! Faithful to the last! Never mentioned old Fagin! And why should they? It wouldn't have saved them from hanging. No, no, no! Fine fellows! Fine fellows!'

With these, and other similar reflections, Fagin replaced the watch in its hiding place. At least half a dozen more were taken out one by one from the same box, and examined with equal pleasure. After that came several rings and other fine articles of jewellery.

As Fagin whispered to himself, his dark eyes fell on Oliver's face; the boy's eyes were fixed on his in silent interest. Fagin closed the lid of the box with a loud crash and, laying his hand on a bread knife which was on the table, jumped up angrily.

'What's that?' said the old man. 'What are you watching me for? Why are you awake? What have you seen? Speak out, boy!'

'I wasn't able to sleep any longer, sir,' replied Oliver. 'I am sorry if I have interrupted you, sir.'

'So you were not awake an hour ago?' said Fagin, looking threateningly at the boy.

'No! No! Indeed!' replied Oliver.

'Are you sure?' cried Fagin, with an even more frightening look than before.

'I promise you I was not, sir,' replied Oliver seriously.

'It's all right, my dear,' said Fagin, suddenly changing his tone and returning to his old manner. He played with the knife a little before he laid it down, as if to make Oliver think that he had picked it up for a joke. 'Of course I know that, my dear. I only tried to frighten you. You're a brave boy. Ha! ha! You're a brave boy, Oliver!' The old man rubbed his hands as he laughed, but looked worried as he glanced at the box.

'Did you see any of those pretty things, my dear?' he asked, laying his hand on it after a short pause.

'Yes, sir,' replied Oliver.

'Ah!' said Fagin, turning rather pale. 'They – they're mine, Oliver; my own property. All I have to live on, in my old age. People call me a miser, my dear. Only a miser, that's all.'

Oliver thought the old man must truly be a miser to live in such a dirty place when he had so many watches. He asked if he could get up.

'Certainly, my dear, certainly,' replied the old gentleman. 'Wait. There's a bowl of water in the corner by the door. Bring it here and you can use it to wash in, my dear.'

Oliver got up, walked across the room and bent for a moment to lift the bowl. When he turned his head, the box had gone.

He had hardly finished washing himself when the Dodger returned, accompanied by a very active young friend whom Oliver had seen smoking on the previous night and who was now introduced to him as Charley Bates. The four sat down to breakfast on the coffee and some hot rolls and meat which the Dodger had brought with him inside his hat.

'Well,' said Fagin, glancing at Oliver, and addressing himself to the Dodger, 'I hope you've been at work this morning, my dears?'

'Hard,' replied the Dodger.

'As nails,' added Charley Bates.

'Good boys, good boys!' said Fagin. 'What have you got, Dodger?'

'A couple of pocketbooks,' replied that young gentleman, producing them.

'Not so heavy as they might be,' said Fagin, after looking at the insides carefully, 'but very neat and nicely made. A clever workman, isn't he, Oliver?'

'Very, indeed, sir,' said Oliver. At which Mr Charley Bates laughed noisily, to the great surprise of Oliver, who saw nothing to laugh at.

'And what have you got, my dear?' said Fagin to Charley Bates.

'Handkerchiefs,' replied Master Bates, producing four.

'Well,' said Fagin, examining them closely, 'they're very good ones. But you haven't marked them well, Charley; so the labels will be picked out with a needle, and we'll teach Oliver how to do it. Shall we, Oliver? Ha! ha! ha!'

'If you please, sir,' said Oliver.

'You'd like to be able to make pocket handkerchiefs as easily as Charley Bates, wouldn't you, my dear?' said the old man.

'Very much indeed, if you'll teach me, sir,' replied Oliver.

Master Bates saw something so funny in this reply that he burst into another laugh and had to struggle to draw breath again.

'He's such a child!' he said, when he recovered.

When the breakfast was cleared away, the cheerful old gentleman and the two boys played a very unusual game, which was performed in this way: the cheerful old gentleman put a snuff-box in one pocket of his trousers, a pocketbook in the other, and a watch in his jacket pocket. He fixed a false diamond pin on his shirt, and, buttoning his coat tightly round him, walked up and down the room with a stick, pretending to be an old man walking around the streets. Sometimes he stopped at the fireplace, and sometimes at the door, apparently staring into shop windows. At such times, he would look around him for fear of thieves, and would keep checking all his pockets in turn to see that he hadn't lost anything. He did this in such a funny manner that Oliver laughed until the tears ran down his face. All this time the two boys followed closely behind him, moving out of his sight so quickly every time he turned round, that it was impossible to follow their movements. At last the Dodger accidentally stepped on his toes, while Charley Bates walked into him from behind and in that one moment they took from him, with most extraordinary speed, snuff-box, pocketbook, shirt pin, pocket handkerchief. If the old gentleman felt a hand in any of the pockets, he shouted out its position; and the game began all over again.

When this game had been played a great many times, a couple of young ladies, one of whom was named Bet and the other Nancy, called to see the young gentlemen. They were untidily dressed, and not exactly pretty, but they were very free and pleasant in their manners and Oliver thought them very nice indeed.

These visitors stayed a long time, drinking spirits and talking happily. At last they went out, accompanied by Charley Bates and the Dodger, having been provided by good old Fagin with money to spend.

'There, my dear,' said the old man, 'that's a pleasant life, isn't it? Make these young gentlemen your models, and take their advice in all matters – especially the Dodger's, my dear. He'll be a great man himself, and will make you one too, if you follow his example. Is my handkerchief hanging out of my pocket, my dear?'

'Yes, sir,' said Oliver.

'See if you can take it out without my feeling it, as you saw them do when we were playing this morning.'

Oliver held up the bottom of the pocket with one hand, as he had seen the Dodger hold it; and drew the handkerchief out with the other hand.

'Is it gone?' cried Fagin.

'Here it is, sir,' said Oliver, showing it in his hand.

'You're a clever boy, my dear,' said the playful old gentleman, stroking Oliver's hair approvingly. 'I never saw a quicker lad. Here are some pennies for you. If you go on in this way, you'll be a great man. And now come here; I'll show you how to take the labels out of the handkerchiefs.'

Oliver wondered how picking the old gentleman's pocket would make him a great man. But thinking that Fagin must know best, he followed him quietly to the table and was soon deeply engaged in his new study.

Chapter 8   Oliver Is Arrested

For many days, Oliver remained in Fagin's room, picking the labels out of the handkerchiefs, and sometimes taking part in the game already described. At last he began to feel the need for fresh air and begged the old gentleman to allow him to go out to work with his two companions.

Finally Fagin agreed to his request and the three boys went out. At first they walked at such a slow pace that Oliver began to think that his companions were not going to work at all. But suddenly the Dodger stopped and pulled his companions back.

'What's the matter?' asked Oliver.

'Quiet!' replied the Dodger. 'Do you see that old man by the bookshop?'

'The old gentleman across the street?' said Oliver. 'Yes, I can see him.'

'He'll do,' said the Dodger.

'A first-class opportunity,' observed Charley Bates.

Oliver looked from one to the other with the greatest surprise; but he was not permitted to make any inquiries, for the two boys walked quickly across the road, closely following the old gentleman. Oliver walked a few steps behind them; and then, not knowing whether to advance or withdraw, stood looking on in silent amazement.

The old gentleman was a very respectable-looking person, with a powdered head and gold glasses. He had picked up a book from the shelf inside the bookshop and there he stood, reading it. He was so involved in his reading that he did not see the shop, the street, or the boys; he saw nothing but his book.

Imagine Oliver's horror and alarm to see the Dodger slip his hand into the old gentleman's pocket, and pull out a handkerchief! To see him hand this to Charley Bates, and finally to see them both running away round the corner at full speed.

The whole mystery of the handkerchiefs, and the watches, and the jewels, and the old man became clear at last in the boy's mind. He stood terrified and confused for a moment, and then he ran away as fast as his legs could carry him.

All this took no more than a minute. At the very moment

when Oliver began to run away, the old gentleman, putting his hand in his pocket and missing his handkerchief, turned sharply round. Seeing Oliver run away at such a rapid pace, he very naturally concluded that he was the robber and, shouting 'Stop thief!' as loudly as he could, ran after him, book in hand.

The Dodger and Bates, hearing the cry and seeing Oliver running, guessed exactly how the matter stood; they stopped running away and, shouting 'Stop thief!' too, they joined in the chase like good citizens.

'Stop thief! Stop thief!' There is a magic in the sound. The cry is taken up by a hundred voices, and the crowd of pursuers increases at every step and turning.

The poor, breathless child ran, with terror in his eyes, until at last they caught him. He fell to the ground, and the crowd gathered eagerly round him, each new arrival struggling with the others for a look. 'Stand aside!' 'Here is the gentleman. Is this the boy, sir?' 'Yes.'

Oliver was lying, covered with mud and dust and bleeding from the mouth, looking wildly round at the faces that surrounded him, when the old gentleman was pushed into the circle by some of the pursuers.

'Yes,' said the gentleman, 'I am afraid it is the boy. Poor fellow! He has hurt himself.'

'I did it, sir,' said a great big fellow, stepping forward. 'I stopped him, sir.'

The fellow touched his hat with a smile, expecting something for his trouble; but the old gentleman looked at him with an expression of dislike, and would have run away himself had not a police officer at that moment made his way through the crowd and seized Oliver by the collar.

'Come, get up,' said the officer roughly.

'It wasn't me, indeed, sir. It was two other boys,' said Oliver, looking round desperately. 'They are here somewhere.'

'Oh, no, they aren't,' said the officer. 'Come on, get up!'

'Don't hurt him,' begged the old gentleman.

'Oh, no, I won't hurt him,' replied the officer, pulling Oliver's jacket half off his back. 'Come, I know you; it won't do. Will you stand upon your feet, you young devil?'

Oliver, who could hardly stand, was dragged along the street by the collar of his coat, at a rapid pace. The gentleman walked on with them by the officer's side; and many of the people in the crowd ran on ahead of them and stared back at Oliver from time to time.

Chapter 9   Oliver Is Released

Oliver and the old gentleman were taken to the office of the magistrate Mr Fang, a thin, hot-tempered man who was in the habit of drinking more than was good for him.

The old gentleman bowed and, advancing to the magistrate's desk, put his card on it, saying: 'That's my name and address, sir.'

But the magistrate was in a bad mood. He looked up angrily from the newspaper he was reading. 'Who are you?' he asked.

The old gentleman pointed, with some surprise, to the card.

'Officer!' said Mr Fang, throwing the card contemptuously away. 'Who is this fellow?'

'My name, sir,' said the old gentleman, 'is Brownlow. Permit me to inquire the name of the magistrate who insults a respectable person while he is supposed to be doing his job.'

'Officer!' said Mr Fang, 'What's this fellow charged with?'

'He's not charged at all, sir,' replied the officer. 'He appears against the boy, sir.'

'Appears against the boy, does he?' said Mr Fang, looking contemptuously at Mr Brownlow from head to foot. 'Swear him in!'

'Before I am sworn in, I must beg to say one word,' said Mr Brownlow; 'and that is, that I really never, without actual experience, could have believed –'

'Hold your tongue, sir!' said Mr Fang.

'I will not, sir!' replied the old gentleman.

'Hold your tongue immediately, or I'll have you turned out of the office!' said Mr Fang. 'Swear this person in!' he added to the clerk.

Mr Brownlow was very angry, but reflecting that he might injure the boy by expressing his anger, he hid his feelings and agreed to be sworn in.

'Now,' said Mr Fang, 'what's the charge against the boy? What have you got to say, sir?'

'I was standing at a bookshop –' Mr Brownlow began.

'Hold your tongue, sir,' said Mr Fang. 'Policeman! Where's the policeman? Here, swear this policeman in. Now, policeman, what is this?'

The policeman related how he had arrested Oliver, and how he had searched him and found nothing on his person.

'Are there any witnesses?' inquired Mr Fang.

'None, sir,' replied the policeman.

Mr Fang was silent for some minutes, and then, turning round angrily to Mr Brownlow, he said: 'Do you mean to state your complaint against this boy, or do you not? You have to tell the truth. Now, if you stand there refusing to give evidence I'll punish you for disrespect to the court.'

With many interruptions, and repeated insults, Mr Brownlow managed to state his case: that, in the surprise of the moment, he had run after the boy because he saw him running away. He begged the magistrate to deal as gently with him as justice would allow.

'He has been hurt already,' said the old gentleman in conclusion. 'And I fear,' he added, 'that he is ill.'

'Oh, yes, I dare say!' said Mr Fang, with a twisted smile. 'Come, none of your tricks here, you little devil, they won't do. What's your name?'

Oliver tried to reply, but his tongue failed him. He was deadly pale; and the whole place seemed to be turning round and round.

The officer, being a kind-hearted man and seeing that Oliver was too weak and afraid to answer for himself, answered the magistrate's questions and told him that he thought the boy was really ill.

But the magistrate sentenced him to three months in prison, with hard labour, and the boy would have been taken away to prison had it not been for the owner of the bookshop, who rushed into the office and at this point advanced towards the bench.

'Stop! Stop! Don't take him away! For heaven's sake stop a moment!' cried the newcomer, breathlessly.

'What's this? Who is this man? Turn him out!' cried Mr Fang.

'I *will* speak,' cried the man. 'I will not be turned out. I saw it all. I run the bookshop. I demand to be sworn in.'

'Swear the man in,' growled Mr Fang. 'Now, man, what have you got to say?'

The bookseller related how he had seen the three boys, the prisoner and two others, waiting on the opposite side of the road while Mr Brownlow was reading. He said that the robbery had been committed by another boy; that Oliver had looked completely amazed by it.

Having listened to his story, the magistrate ordered the boy to be released and the office to be cleared.

A coach was found and Oliver was laid carefully on one seat, the old gentleman got in and sat on the other, and away the coach drove to Mr Brownlow's house.

Chapter 10   Oliver Stays at Mr Brownlow's

At Mr Brownlow's house, a bed was quickly prepared for Oliver and he was carefully and comfortably laid in it; here he was looked after with a kindness that he had never before experienced.

But for many days Oliver remained unaware of all the goodness of his new friends. He lay in his bed, burning from the heat of a fever. When at last he awoke from what seemed to have been a long and troubled dream, he was weak, thin and pale. Raising himself in the bed, with his head resting on his trembling arm, he looked anxiously around.

'What room is this? Where have I been brought?' said Oliver.

A motherly old lady who had been sitting at his bedside rose as she heard these words and said to him softly: 'Ssh, my dear. You must be very quiet, or you will be ill again. Lie down again, there's a dear!'

Oliver obeyed, partly to please the old lady, who was so kind to him, and partly because he was still very weak. He soon fell into a gentle sleep, from which he was awoken by the light of a candle to see a doctor measure his heartbeat and hear him say that he was a great deal better.

The doctor told Mrs Bedwin, the kind old lady, to give the child a little tea and some dry bread, and not to keep him too warm or too cold. Then he went away.

Oliver fell asleep again. When he woke, it had been a bright day for hours and he felt cheerful and happy. The most dangerous part of the disease had passed. He was going to live. In three days' time he was able to sit in a soft chair and, as he was still too weak to walk, Mrs Bedwin had him carried downstairs to her room, where she set him by the fireside.

The old gentleman, Mr Brownlow, came to see him. 'How do you feel, my dear?' he said.

'Very happy, sir,' said Oliver. 'And very grateful indeed, sir, for your goodness to me.'

'Good boy,' said Mr Brownlow. 'Have you given him any food, Mrs Bedwin?'

'He has just had a bowl of good strong soup, sir,' she replied.

After a few more questions and a little conversation with Oliver, Mr Brownlow went away.

They were happy days, those of Oliver's recovery. Everything was so quiet, neat and orderly. Everybody was kind and gentle. He was no sooner strong enough to put his clothes on than Mr Brownlow had a complete new suit, a new cap and a new pair of shoes bought for him.

One evening Mr Brownlow sent for Oliver to come and talk to him in his study. Mr Brownlow was seated at a table, reading. When he saw Oliver, he pushed the book away from him, and told him to come near the table and sit down. Oliver did so and stared with amazement at the bookshelves that reached from the floor to the ceiling.

'There are a good many books, are there not, my boy?' said Mr Brownlow.

'A great number, sir,' replied Oliver. 'I never saw so many.'

'You shall read them, if you behave well,' said the old gentleman kindly, 'and you will like that better than looking at their covers. How would you like to grow up a clever man and write books?'

'I think I would rather read them, sir,' replied Oliver.

'Now,' said Mr Brownlow in a more serious manner, 'I want you to pay great attention, my boy, to what I am going to say. I shall talk to you without any reserve, because I am sure you are as well able to understand me as many older persons would be.'

'Oh, don't tell me you are going to send me away, sir, please!' cried Oliver, alarmed at the serious tone of Mr Brownlow. 'Don't turn me out to wander in the streets again. Let me stay here and be your servant. Take pity on a poor boy, sir!'

'My dear child,' said the old gentleman, moved by the warmth of Oliver's sudden appeal, 'you need not be afraid that I will abandon you, unless you give me reason to.'

'I never, never will, sir,' promised Oliver.

'I hope not,' said the old gentleman. 'I do not think you ever will. I feel confident that I can trust you. You say you are an orphan, without a friend in the world; all the inquiries I have been able to make confirm this statement. Let me hear your story: where you came from; who brought you up; and how you got into the company in which I found you. Speak the truth, and you shall not be friendless while I live.'

Oliver began to tell his sad story. While he was doing so an old friend of Mr Brownlow, called Mr Grimwig, arrived. Mr Grimwig was a heavy old gentleman, rather lame in one leg, and he walked with the support of a thick stick. He had a way of twisting his head to one side when he spoke, and of looking out of the corners of his eyes at the same time, which reminded one of some kind of bird. He took up this position the moment he made his appearance and, holding out a small piece of orange peel at arm's length, he complained: 'Look here! Do you see this! Isn't it a most extraordinary thing that I can't call at a friend's house without finding a piece of orange peel on the stairs? I've already been made lame with orange peel, and I know orange peel will kill me one day, or I'll eat my own head, sir!'

This was Mr Grimwig's strange way of confirming nearly every statement he made.

'I'll eat my head, sir,' repeated Mr Grimwig, striking his stick upon the ground. 'Hullo! What's that?' he said suddenly, looking at Oliver and taking a step or two backwards.

'This is young Oliver Twist, whom we were speaking about,' said Mr Brownlow.

Oliver bowed.

'You don't mean to say that's the boy who had the fever, I hope?' said Mr Grimwig, moving back a little further. 'Wait a minute! Don't speak! Stop!' continued Mr Grimwig, losing all fear of the fever in his excitement at the discovery. 'That's the boy who had the orange! If that's not the boy, sir, who had the orange and threw this bit of peel down on the staircase, I'll eat my head and his too.'

'No, no, he has not had an orange,' said Mr Brownlow, laughing. 'Come! Put down your hat, and speak to my young friend.'

'I feel strongly on this subject, sir,' said the old gentleman. 'There's always orange peel in our street; and I *know* it's put there by the assistant of the doctor at the corner.'

Then, putting on his eye-glasses, he looked at Oliver who, seeing that he was the object of inspection, reddened and bowed again.

'How are you, boy?' said Mr Grimwig, eventually.

'A great deal better, thank you, sir,' replied Oliver.

Mr Brownlow asked Oliver to step downstairs and tell Mrs Bedwin they were ready for tea.

'He is a nice-looking boy, is he not?' inquired Mr Brownlow.

'I don't know,' replied Mr Grimwig. 'Where does he come from? Who is he? What is he? He has had a fever. What of that? People are not good just because they have a fever, are they?'

Now, the fact was that in his own heart Mr Grimwig also felt that Oliver was a nice-looking and good-mannered boy; but he always liked to be different. Mr Brownlow, knowing his friend's strange habits well, accepted his opposition with good humour. And so everything went very smoothly at tea and Oliver, who was invited to remain with the two gentlemen, began to feel more relaxed.

'And when are you going to hear a full and true account of the life and adventures of Oliver Twist?' asked Mr Grimwig of

Mr Brownlow, at the end of the meal, looking sideways at Oliver.

'Tomorrow morning,' replied Mr Brownlow. 'Come up to see me tomorrow morning at ten o clock, Oliver.'

'Yes, sir,' replied Oliver. He answered after a short pause, because he was confused by Mr Grimwig's looking hard at him.

'I'll tell you what,' whispered the gentleman to Mr Brownlow, 'he won't come up to you tomorrow morning. I saw him think about it. He is deceiving you, my good friend.'

'I'll swear he is not,' replied Mr Brownlow, warmly.

'If he is not,' said Mr Grimwig, 'I'll eat my head.'

'We shall see,' said Mr Brownlow, struggling to control his rising anger.

'We will,' replied Mr Grimwig, with an annoying smile, 'we will.'

At this moment, Mrs Bedwin happened to bring in a small parcel of books which Mr Brownlow had that morning bought at the same bookshop where his pocket had been picked.

'Stop the shop-boy, Mrs Bedwin!' said Mr Brownlow. 'There is something to go back.' But the boy had gone.

'Send Oliver with the books,' said Mr Grimwig, with a knowing smile. 'He will be sure to deliver them safely, you know.'

'Yes, do let me take them, if you please, sir,' said Oliver. 'I'll run all the way, sir.'

'You shall go, my dear,' said the old man. 'The books are on a chair by my table. Fetch them down.'

Oliver, delighted to be of use, brought the books down and waited to hear what message he was to take.

'You are to say,' said Mr Brownlow, looking steadily at Grimwig, 'you are to say that you have brought those books back; and that you have come to pay the four pounds ten I owe them. This is a five-pound note, so you will have to bring me back the change.'

'I won't be ten minutes, sir,' said Oliver, and having buttoned up the bank note in his coat pocket and placed the books carefully under his arm, he made a respectful bow and left the room. Mrs Bedwin followed him to the door, giving him many directions about the best way to go, the name of the bookseller and the name of the street. Having told him to be sure and not catch cold, the old lady finally permitted him to leave.

'What a lovely child!' said the old lady, looking after him. 'I can't bear, somehow, to let him out of my sight.'

At this moment, Oliver looked cheerfully round and waved before he turned the corner. The old lady smilingly returned his wave, and, closing the door, went back to her own room.

'Let me see; he'll be back in twenty minutes at the longest,' said Mr Brownlow, pulling out his watch and placing it on the table.

'Oh! You really expect him to come back, do you?' inquired Mr Grimwig.

'Don't you?' asked Mr Brownlow, smiling.

The spirit of argument was strong in Mr Grimwig's breast at the moment; and it was strengthened by his friend's confident smile.

'No,' he said, banging the table. 'I do not. The boy has a new suit of clothes on his back, a set of valuable books under his arm, and a five-pound note in his pocket. He'll join his old friends the thieves and laugh at you. If ever that boy returns to this house, sir, I'll eat my head.'

With these words he pulled his chair closer to the table; and there the two friends sat in silent expectation, with the watch between them. It grew dark so that the figures on the watch face could hardly be seen, but there the two gentlemen continued to sit, in silence, with the watch between them.

Chapter 11   In Fagin's Hands Once More

'Where's Oliver?' said the old man, rising with a threatening look on seeing the Dodger and Charley Bates without him. 'Where's the boy?'

The young thieves looked anxiously at each other, but they did not reply.

'What's happened to the boy?' said Fagin, seizing the Dodger tightly by his collar and shaking him violently. 'Speak out, or I'll kill you!'

'The police have got him, and that's all there is to tell,' said the Dodger angrily. 'Come, let go of me, will you!'

Pulling himself out of the big coat, which he left in Fagin's hand, the Dodger picked up the bread knife and would have pushed it into the old man's chest if the latter had not stepped back in time. Then, seizing up a pot of beer, Fagin prepared to throw it at the Dodger's head but, the Dodger avoiding the pot in time, the beer hit another member of the gang who had just arrived.

It was Bill Sikes, followed by his dog. Bill was a strongly built fellow of about thirty-five years of age with an angry-looking face and a beard of three days' growth.

'Who threw that beer at me? It is well it is the beer, and not the pot which hit me, or I'd have killed somebody. I might have known that nobody but a rich, miserly old man like you could afford to throw away any drink but water. What is it all about, Fagin? What are you up to? Ill-treating the boys, you greedy old thief? I'm surprised they don't murder you. I would, if I was in their place.'

'Quietly! Quietly! Mr Sikes!' said the old man, trembling. 'Don't speak so loudly.'

'Don't you call me "Mr",' replied the villain. 'You always mean trouble when you call me "Mr". You know my name: out with it.'

'Well, well, then – Bill Sikes,' agreed Fagin. 'You seem to be in a bad mood, Bill.'

'Perhaps I am,' replied Sikes, and then he demanded a drink. 'And be careful you don't poison it,' he added, putting his hat on the table.

The young thieves told Sikes how Oliver Twist had been captured and how the police had arrested him.

'I'm afraid,' said Fagin, 'that he may say something which may get us into trouble.'

'That's very likely,' replied Sikes.

'And I'm afraid, you see,' added Fagin, 'that if we are caught, there are a good many more people who are likely to be locked up at the same time – and for rather longer.'

'Somebody must find out what has happened at the magistrate's office,' said Sikes.

The old man nodded agreement.

The wisdom of this plan was obvious; but unfortunately neither Fagin, nor Sikes, nor the Dodger, nor Bates had any desire to go near a police station. Later, though, the two young ladies whom Oliver had seen on a former occasion entered the room.

'The very thing!' said Fagin. 'Bet will go, won't you, my dear?'

'Where?' inquired the young lady.

'Only just up to the magistrate's office, my dear.'

Bet refused to go, and Fagin turned to Nancy.

'Nancy, my dear,' he said, 'what do you say?'

'That I shan't go either,' said she.

'She'll go, Fagin,' said Sikes.

And Mr Sikes was right. By threats and promises Nancy was at last persuaded to accept the task.

She made her way to the police station and when she came to the police officer she burst into tears and began to cry, apparently in great unhappiness, saying: 'Oh, my brother! What has happened to him? Where is he? Where have they taken him? Oh! Do have pity and tell me what's been done with the dear boy, if you please, sir!'

The officer informed the deeply affected sister that Oliver had been taken ill in the office and released because a witness had proved the robbery to have been committed by another boy. He told her that the gentleman who had accused Oliver had taken him away to his own house, somewhere in Pentonville.

In a terrible state of uncertainty the young woman walked to the gate, and then she ran as fast as she could, by the most complicated route she could think of, to Fagin's house.

Mr Bill Sikes no sooner heard her account than he called his dog and left quickly.

Fagin instructed Nancy, Charley and the Dodger to watch and listen near the house until they brought home some news of Oliver. He unlocked a drawer and gave them some money, telling them that he would shut his house that night, and that they knew where to find him.

Then he pushed them from the room and, carefully locking the door behind them, he took from its hiding place the box which Oliver had seen him examine. He quickly removed the watches and the jewellery and, hiding them under his clothes, he left the house.

♦

Oliver Twist was on his way to the bookshop. He was walking along, thinking how fortunate he was, when he was surprised by a young woman screaming loudly, 'Oh, my dear brother!' He looked up to see what the matter was, and a pair of arms was thrown tightly around his neck.

'Don't!' said Oliver, struggling. 'Let go of me. Who are you? What are you stopping me for?'

The only reply to this was more loud screams from the young woman who had seized him. They were answered by the arrival of a cruel-looking man, whom Nancy, for the young woman was Nancy, addressed by the name of Bill Sikes. He was closely followed by his dog.

It was dark now; they were in a poor neighbourhood; no help was near; it was useless for Oliver to struggle. In another moment he was dragged into an area of dark, narrow streets, and was pushed along them at such speed that his cries went unheard.

◆

Meanwhile, in Mr Brownlow's house, the gas-lamps were lit; Mrs Bedwin was waiting anxiously at the open door; the servant had run up the street twenty times to see if there was any sign of Oliver; and still the two old gentlemen sat with the watch between them.

◆

The narrow streets finally ended in a large open space. Having crossed that, Oliver's guards turned into a very dirty narrow street, lined with used clothes shops. The dog ran forward and stopped before the door of a shop that was closed and apparently unoccupied; the house was in a poor state of repair and on the door was nailed a TO LET sign which looked as if it had hung there for many years.

'All right,' cried Sikes, looking carefully around him.

Nancy reached out, and Oliver heard the sound of a bell. They crossed to the opposite side of the street and stood for a few moments under a lamp. A little window was opened; soon afterwards the door softly opened. Mr Sikes then seized the terrified boy by the collar, and all three were soon inside the house.

The passage was perfectly dark. They waited while the person who had let them in chained and bolted the door.

'Is Fagin here?' asked the robber.

'Yes,' replied the voice. 'Won't he be glad to see you!'

The style of this reply, as well as the voice which spoke it, seemed familiar to Oliver's ears; in fact it was the Artful Dodger, who soon lit a candle and led them in. They crossed an empty kitchen, and, opening the door to a small back room, they were received with a shout of laughter.

'Oh, Fagin, look at him! Fagin, do look at him! I can't bear it; it is such an entertaining game, I can't bear it. Hold me, somebody, while I laugh it out.'

It was Master Bates who, unable to control his amusement, lay flat on the floor and laughed noisily for five minutes.

The old man, taking off his nightcap, made a great number of low bows to the amazed boy. Meanwhile, the Artful Dodger was busy picking Oliver's pockets.

'Look at his suit, Fagin!' said Charley Bates 'And his books, too!'

'Delighted to see you looking so well, my dear,' said the old Jew, bowing with a respect that was rather less than genuine. 'The Artful Dodger shall give you another suit, my dear; we don't want you to spoil that Sunday one. Why didn't you write, my dear, and say you were coming? We'd have got something warm for supper.'

At this Master Bates shouted with laughter again, so loudly that Fagin himself relaxed and even the Dodger smiled. At that moment the Dodger pulled out the five-pound note.

'Hullo! What's that?' inquired Sikes, stepping forward as Fagin seized the note. 'That's mine.'

'No, no, my dear,' said Fagin. 'Mine, Bill, mine. You shall have the books.'

'If that isn't mine,' said Bill Sikes, putting on his hat with a determined air, 'mine and Nancy's, that is, I'll take the boy back again.'

The old man stared at him.

'Come on! Hand it over, will you?' said Sikes.

'This is hardly fair, Bill; hardly fair, is it, Nancy?' inquired Fagin.

'Fair or not fair,' replied Sikes, 'hand it over, I tell you. Do you think Nancy and me have got nothing else to do with our time than to spend it capturing every young boy who gets caught through you? Give it here, you greedy old thief, give it here.'

With these words Sikes took the note from between the old man's finger and thumb and tied it in his handkerchief. He told Fagin he could keep the books, if he was fond of reading; if not, he could sell them.

'They belong to the old gentleman,' said Oliver, finding his voice at last. 'To the kind old gentleman who took me into his house, and had me nursed when I was nearly dying of the fever. Oh, please send them back; send him back the books and money. He'll think I stole them; the old lady, too; she will think I stole them. Oh, do take pity on me, and send them back.'

With these words Oliver fell on his knees at the old man's feet.

'The boy is right,' remarked Fagin. 'You're right, Oliver, you're right; they *will* think you have stolen them. Ha! ha! It couldn't have turned out better.'

'Of course it couldn't,' replied Sikes. 'I knew that as soon as I saw him coming with the books under his arm. They're soft-hearted people, or they wouldn't have taken him in at all; and they'll ask no questions about him in case they have to have him arrested and brought before a court of law. He's safe enough.'

On hearing these words Oliver jumped suddenly to his feet and ran out of the room, shouting for help.

'Keep back the dog, Bill!' cried Nancy, jumping to the door and closing it, as Fagin and his two pupils rushed out after him. 'Keep back the dog; he'll pull the boy to pieces.'

'That serves him right!' cried Sikes, struggling to free himself from the girl. 'Stand away from me, or I'll split your head against the wall.'

He pushed the girl from him to the far end of the room, just as Fagin and the two boys returned, dragging Oliver behind them.

'So you wanted to run away, my dear, did you?' said Fagin, taking up a short heavy stick which lay in a corner of the fireplace.

Oliver did not reply, but he watched the old man's movements, and breathed quickly.

'Wanted to get help; called for the police, did you?' said Fagin, catching the boy by the arm. 'We'll cure you of that, my young master.'

He gave Oliver a hard blow on the shoulders with the stick, and was raising it for a second stroke when the girl, rushing forward, pulled it from his hand and threw it violently into the fire.

'You've got the boy,' cried the girl. 'What more do you want? Leave him alone – leave him alone, or I'll kill you.'

'What do you mean by this?' said Sikes. 'Do you know who you are, and what you are?'

'Oh, yes, I know all about that,' replied the girl.

'Well, then, keep quiet,' ordered Sikes, 'or I'll quiet you for a good long time to come. You're a nice one, to discover human feelings and make a friend of the boy!'

'God help me!' cried the girl, 'and I wish I had been struck dead in the street before I lent a hand in bringing him here. He's a thief, a liar, a devil, all that's bad, from this night on. Isn't that enough for the old man, without hitting him too?'

'Come, come,' said Fagin, 'we must have polite words; polite words.'

'Polite words!' cried the girl, whose anger was terrible to see. 'Polite words, you villain! Yes, you deserve them from me. I robbed for you when I was a child not half as old as he is!' she added, pointing to Oliver. 'I have been in the same trade for twelve years, don't you know it? Speak out! Don't you know it?'

'Well, well,' replied Fagin, 'and if you have, it's your living!'

'Well yes, it is!' returned the girl. 'It is my living; and the cold, wet, dirty streets are my home; and you're the villain that drove me to them long ago, and that will keep me there, day and night, till I die!'

'I shall do you more harm than that,' said Fagin, 'if you say any more!'

The girl said nothing more, but ran at the old man and would have done him serious damage if her wrists had not been seized by Sikes just in time. She struggled unsuccessfully to free herself, and then she fainted.

Chapter 12   Oliver Is to Take Part in a Robbery

At around midday the next day, when the Dodger and Bates had gone out, Mr Fagin gave Oliver a long lecture on the ungratefulness he had shown in trying to run away from his friends. He reminded him that he had taken him in and given him shelter and protection. He also told him the story of another young lad whom Fagin had caused to be hanged because he had tried to inform on them to the police.

Little Oliver's blood ran cold as he listened to these words and tried to understand the dark threats they carried.

The old man, smiling in his ugly manner, ran his fingers through Oliver's hair and said that if he kept quiet and did what he was told to do they could still be very good friends. Then, taking his hat and covering himself with an old overcoat, Fagin went out and locked the door behind him.

And so Oliver remained that day, and for the greater part of many days after that, seeing nobody between early morning and midnight, and left during the long hours to his own sad thoughts.

One cold, wet, windy night Fagin wrapped himself tightly in his overcoat and, pulling the collar up over his ears to hide the lower part of his face completely, left his home. He walked along the dark, muddy streets until he came to where Bill Sikes lived.

The dog growled as the old man touched the handle of the front door, and Bill demanded to know who was there.

'Only me, Bill; only me, my dear,' said Fagin, looking in.

'Come in, then,' said Sikes. 'Lie down, you stupid animal. Don't you know the devil when he's got an overcoat on? Well!'

'Well, my dear,' replied the old man. 'Ah! Nancy.' The young lady, who was sitting by the fire, told him to pull up a chair.

'It *is* cold, Nancy dear,' said Fagin, as he warmed his hands over the fire. 'It seems to go right through one,' added the old man, touching his side.

'Give him something to drink, Nancy. Now then, I'm ready; say what you've got to say.'

'About the house at Chertsey. When is it to be done, Bill? When is it to be done? Such silver, my dear, such silver!' said Fagin, rubbing his hands.

'Toby Crackit has been hanging about the place for a fortnight, and he can't get one of the servants to help us. The old lady has employed them for twenty years now, and if you were to give them five hundred pounds, they wouldn't help us.'

'It's a sad thing,' said Fagin, 'to lose so much when we had set our hearts on it.'

'So it is,' said Sikes. 'Worse luck!' After a long silence, Sikes suddenly added: 'Fagin, will you give me fifty pounds extra, if it's safely done from the outside?'

'Yes,' said Fagin.

'Then,' said Sikes, 'we'll do it as soon as you like. Toby and me went over the garden wall last night, to examine the door and the windows. The house is secured at night like a prison; but there's one part we can break through safely.'

'Which is that, Bill?' asked Fagin eagerly.

'Never mind which part it is,' said Sikes. 'You can't do it without me, I know; but it's best to be on the safe side when one deals with you.'

'As you like, my dear, as you like. Is there no help needed, but yours and Toby's?'

'None,' said Sikes, 'except a boy; you must find us a little boy.'

'Oliver's the boy for you, my dear,' replied Fagin in a whisper. 'He's been in good training these last few weeks, and it's time he began to work for his bread. Besides, the others are all too big.'

'Well, he is just the size I want,' said Mr Sikes.

'And he will do everything you want, Bill, my dear,' interrupted Fagin, 'if you frighten him enough.'

'Frighten him!' repeated Sikes. 'If he doesn't obey, you won't see him alive again, Fagin. Think of that, before you send him.'

'I've thought of it all,' said the old man. 'I've had my eye upon him, my dears. As soon as we make him feel that he is one of us; when we fill his mind with the idea that he has been a thief – then he's ours! Ours for his life.'

'When is it to be done?' asked Nancy.

'I planned with Toby the night after tomorrow,' replied Sikes, 'if he heard nothing else from me.'

'Good,' said Fagin. 'There's no moon.'

'No,' replied Sikes. 'You'd better bring the boy here tomorrow night. I shall leave here an hour after daybreak.'

After some discussion it was decided that Nancy should go to Fagin's house next evening and bring Oliver back with her, since Fagin remarked that the boy would be more willing to accompany the girl who had so recently spoken up for him than anybody else.

He looked closely at Nancy before he took his leave. Then he returned to his dark little house where the Dodger was sitting up, waiting for his return.

Chapter 13   The Attempt

When Oliver woke the next morning, Fagin told him that he was to be taken to the house of Bill Sikes that night.

'To – to – stay there, sir?' asked Oliver, anxiously.

'No, no, my dear. Not to stay there,' replied the old man. 'Don't be afraid, Oliver, you shall come back to us. I suppose you want to know what you're going to Bill's for – eh, my dear?'

'Yes, sir, I want to know,' replied Oliver.

'Wait till Bill tells you, then,' said Fagin.

At night Fagin gave him a candle to burn and a book to read, and told him to wait until they came to fetch him. Then he said to him: 'Be careful, Oliver! Bill is a rough man, and stops at nothing when he is angry. Whatever happens, say nothing and do what he tells you.'

Having given him this warning, Fagin left the house.

Oliver was confused about the real purpose and meaning of Fagin's words. He remained lost in thought for some minutes; and then he picked up the book which the old man had left him and began to read. The book was all about crime and great criminals. He read of terrible crimes that made his blood run cold. The descriptions were so real that the pages seemed to turn red with the blood, and the words on them sounded in his ears as if they were whispered by the spirits of the dead.

Overcome with fear, the boy closed the book and pushed it away from him. Then, falling on his knees, he prayed to God to spare him from such actions and to save him from his present dangers.

He had finished his prayer, but still remained with his head buried in his hands, when he heard a slight noise.

'What's that!' he cried, jumping up. 'Who's there?'

'Me. Only me,' replied a trembling voice.

Oliver raised the candle above his head, and looked towards

the door. It was Nancy.

'Put down the light,' said the girl, turning away her head. 'It hurts my eyes.'

Oliver saw that she was very pale, and gently inquired if she was ill. The girl threw herself into a chair, but did not reply.

'God forgive me!' she cried after a while, 'I never thought of this.'

The girl beat her hands upon her knees and shook with cold. Oliver added wood to the fire.

'Nancy!' he cried. 'What is it?'

Pulling her chair close to the fire, she sat there for a while without speaking; finally she raised her head and looked round.

'I don't know what comes over me sometimes,' she said. 'It's this cold, dirty room, I think. Now, Nolly, dear, are you ready?'

'Am I to go with you?' asked Oliver.

'Yes. I have come from Bill,' replied the girl. 'You are to go with me.'

'What for?' asked Oliver, moving away from her.

'What for?' repeated the girl, raising her eyes but avoiding looking at Oliver. 'Oh, for no harm.'

'I don't believe it,' said Oliver, who had watched her closely.

'Have it your own way,' replied the girl, pretending to laugh. 'For no good, then.'

Oliver could see that he had some power over the girl's better feelings and for a moment thought of appealing to her pity for his helpless state. But then it occurred to him that it was not yet eleven o'clock, and that many people were still in the streets who might help him to get free. He stepped forward and said that he was ready.

The girl eyed him carefully; she had guessed what had been passing through his mind.

'I have saved you from being ill-treated once,' she reminded him, 'and I will again, and I do now. I have promised that you will

47

be quiet; if you are not, you will only do harm to yourself, and to me, and perhaps be my death. I have suffered all this for you already.'

She pointed quickly at the bruises on her neck and arms, and continued: 'Remember this! And don't let me suffer any more for you just now. If I could help you, I would, but I do not have the power. Now give me your hand. Hurry! Your hand!'

She caught Oliver's hand and, blowing out the candle, pulled him behind her up the stairs. The door was opened quickly by someone unseen in the darkness, and was as quickly closed when they had passed out. A carriage was waiting; the girl pulled Oliver in with her, and drew the curtains. The driver needed no directions; he whipped his horse into full speed. The carriage stopped at Bill Sikes's house. In a moment they were inside, and the door was shut.

'Hullo!' replied Sikes, appearing at the head of the stairs with a candle. 'Oh! Come on up! So you've got the child. Did he come quietly?'

'Like a lamb,' said Nancy.

'I'm glad to hear it,' said Sikes, looking severely at Oliver, 'for his own sake. Come here, my boy, and listen to what I'm going to say.'

Mr Sikes, taking Oliver by the shoulder, sat down by a table and stood the boy in front of him.

'Now, first: do you know what this is?' inquired Sikes, picking up a small pistol which lay on the table.

'Yes, sir,' said Oliver.

'Well, then, look here,' continued Sikes. 'This is powder, and this is a bullet.' Then, having loaded the pistol, he seized Oliver's wrist and put the barrel so close to his head that they touched. 'If you speak a word,' he said, 'when you're out with me, except when I speak to you, that bullet will be in your head. So if you do make up your mind to speak without permission, say your prayers first. And now, Nancy, let's have some supper and get some sleep before we start.'

It was a grey, unpleasant morning when they got out into the street; strong winds were blowing, it was raining hard, and the clouds were looking dull and stormy.

Mr Bill Sikes, holding Oliver firmly by the hand, hurried on through the streets of the great city and along the country roads which eventually took their place.

It was quite dark when, through narrow lanes and across muddy fields, they came to a lonely and decaying house. No light could be seen from the windows; the house seemed to be empty. A little pressure on the door from Sikes's hand opened it and they passed in together.

'Hullo,' cried a loud, rough voice, as soon as they set foot in the passage.

'Don't make such a noise,' said Sikes, bolting the door. 'Show a light, Toby.'

It was Toby Crackit, who specialized in breaking into private houses.

They entered a low, dark room with a smoky fire, a table, and two or three broken chairs.

'Bill, my boy!' said Mr Crackit. 'I'm glad to see you. I was almost afraid you'd given up the idea, in which case I would have made the attempt without your help. Hullo!' His shout of surprise came as his eye rested on Oliver. Mr Toby Crackit demanded to know who the boy was.

'The boy. Only the boy,' replied Sikes. 'Now, if you'll give us something to eat and drink while we're waiting, you'll put some heart in us.'

'Here,' said Toby, placing some food and a bottle on the table. 'Success to the attempt!' He filled a glass with spirits, and drank down its contents. Mr Sikes did the same.

At half past one they put on their coats. Toby, opening a

cupboard, brought out a pair of loaded pistols, which he pushed into his pockets.

'Now, then,' he said, 'is everything ready? Nothing forgotten?'

'All right,' said Sikes, holding Oliver by the hand. 'Take his other hand, Toby.'

The two robbers went out with Oliver between them. It was now very dark. The mist was much thicker than it had been in the early part of the night. They crossed a bridge and soon arrived at the little town of Chertsey. They hurried through the main street, which at that late hour was completely deserted. Then they turned up a road to the left. After walking about a quarter of a mile they stopped in front of a house surrounded by a wall, to the top of which Toby Crackit, hardly pausing to take breath, climbed in a second.

'The boy next,' said Toby. 'Lift him up; I'll catch hold of him.'

Before Oliver had time to look round, Sikes had caught him under the arms; and in three or four seconds he and Toby were lying on the grass on the other side. Sikes followed immediately, and they walked quietly towards the house.

And now for the first time Oliver understood that robbery, if not murder, was the object of their journey. A mist came before his eyes; his legs failed him, and he sank down on his knees.

'Get up,' whispered Sikes, trembling with anger, and taking the pistol out of his pocket. 'Get up, or I'll scatter your brains across the grass.'

'Oh! For God's sake let me go!' cried Oliver. 'Let me run away and die in the fields. I will never come near London; never, never! Oh! Please take pity on me, and do not make me steal.'

Sikes swore and would have fired the pistol if Toby had not knocked it from his hand and, putting his hand over the boy's mouth, dragged him to the house.

'Quiet!' cried Toby. 'Say another word and I'll knock you down with a crack on the head. That makes no noise, and is quite as certain as a bullet. Here, Bill, force the window open.'

After some delay, and some assistance from Toby, the window was open. It was a little window about five and a half feet above the ground, at the back of the house. The owners had probably not thought it worth securing more efficiently, but it was large enough to admit a boy of Oliver's size.

'Now listen,' whispered Sikes, drawing a candle from his pocket. 'I'm going to put you through there. Take this light; go softly up the steps straight before you, and along the little hall to the street door; unlock it, and let us in.'

Now Toby stood firmly with his head against the wall beneath the window, and his hands on his knees, to make a step out of his back. As soon as this was done, Sikes, climbing on his back, put Oliver gently through the window with his feet first and, without letting go of his collar, planted him safely on the floor inside.

'Take this candle,' said Sikes, looking into the room. 'You can see the stairs in front of you.'

'Yes,' whispered Oliver, more dead than alive.

Sikes, pointing to the front door with his pistol, reminded him that he was within range of the gun all the way; and that if he paused for a second, he would fall dead.

'It's done in a minute,' said Sikes, in the same low whisper. 'As soon as I let you go, do your work. Listen!'

'What's that?' whispered the other man.

They listened carefully.

'Nothing,' said Sikes, releasing his hold on Oliver. 'Now!'

In the short time he had to collect his senses, the boy had firmly resolved that, whether he died in the attempt or not, he would make one effort to rush upstairs from the hall and warn the family. With this idea in mind, he advanced at once.

'Come back!' suddenly cried Sikes. 'Back! Back!'

Frightened by the sudden noise in the silence of the night and by a loud cry which followed it, Oliver let his candle fall. He did not know whether to go on or run away.

The cry was repeated – a light appeared – a vision of two terrified half-dressed men at the top of the stairs swam before his eyes – there was a flash – a loud noise – smoke – a crash somewhere.

Sikes had disappeared for a moment; but he was up again, and had Oliver by the collar once more. He fired his own pistol after the men, who were already withdrawing, and dragged the boy towards the window.

'Hold on to me tighter,' said Sikes, as he pulled him through the window. 'They've hit him. How the boy bleeds!'

Then came the loud ringing of a bell, mixed with shouts and the noise of pistols, and the feeling of being carried over uneven ground at a rapid pace. And then the noises grew confused and a cold, deadly feeling came over the boy's heart – and he saw and heard no more.

Chapter 14   Mr Giles Catches a Thief!

The noise of their pursuers grew louder as Sikes rested the body of the wounded boy on a piece of dry ground. The men were already climbing the gate of the field in which he stood, and a couple of dogs were just in front of them.

'It's all over, Bill!' cried Toby. 'Leave the boy and run!' With this parting advice, Mr Crackit turned and ran at full speed. Sikes took one look around, threw his coat over Oliver and, running along the fence for some distance, he was over it in one jump and was gone.

The three pursuers called back their dogs and stopped to consult with each other.

'My advice is,' said the fattest man in the party, 'that we immediately go home again.'

'I agree with you, Mr Giles,' said a shorter man called Mr Brittles, who was very pale and frightened. In fact all three men were afraid, although they were ashamed to admit it at first.

Mr Giles was head servant to the old lady of the house where the robbery had been attempted. Brittles was a lad of all work who, having entered her service as a mere child, was treated as a young boy still, although he was now past thirty. The third man was a travelling tinker, who had joined in the chase with his two dogs.

Encouraging each other with conversation, and keeping very close together, the three men returned home at a good pace.

The air grew colder as the new day approached, and the mist rolled along the ground like a thick cloud of smoke. Oliver still lay motionless and unconscious in the place where Sikes had left him.

Morning arrived fast. The rain came down thick and hard, but Oliver did not feel it as it beat against him; for he still lay stretched out on his bed of clay.

Finally the boy woke up, crying out in pain. His left arm hung heavy and useless at his side. He was so weak that he could hardly sit up, but he managed at last to stand and then walk unsteadily, although he had no idea where he was going. He continued on until he reached a road and, looking around him, saw a house at no great distance, towards which he directed his steps in the hope of getting assistance. He walked across the grass, climbed the steps, knocked faintly at the door, and then, his whole strength failing him, he sank down on the doorstep.

It happened about this time that Mr Giles, Brittles and the tinker were having tea in the kitchen. Mr Giles was giving his hearers (including the cook and housemaid) a detailed account of the robbery, to which they listened with breathless interest.

'It was about half past two,' said Mr Giles, 'when I woke up and thought I heard a noise.'

53

At this point in the story, the cook turned pale and asked the housemaid to shut the door; the housemaid asked Brittles, and Brittles asked the tinker, who pretended not to hear.

'I heard a noise,' continued Mr Giles. 'At first I said to myself, this is only your imagination, Giles, and I was preparing to fall asleep again when I heard the noise distinctly once again.'

'Good Lord!' cried the cook and housemaid at the same time, moving their chairs closer together.

'I heard it now, quite distinctly,' Mr Giles continued. 'Somebody, I said to myself, is forcing a door or a window; what's to be done? I'll call up that poor lad Brittles, and save him from being murdered in his bed, or having his throat cut.'

Here all eyes were turned on Brittles, who stared at the speaker with his mouth wide open and his face a perfect expression of horror.

'I threw off the bedclothes,' said Giles, 'got softly out of bed, seized a loaded pistol and walked on the tips of my toes to his room. "Brittles," I said, when I had woken him, "don't be frightened!" '

'So you did,' confirmed Brittles, in a low voice.

'Was he frightened?' asked the cook.

'Not a bit of it,' replied Mr Giles. 'He was as firm – ah! nearly as firm as I was.'

'I would have died at once, I'm sure, if it had been me,' observed the housemaid.

'You're a woman,' said Brittles.

'Brittles is right,' said Mr Giles, nodding his head approvingly; 'from a woman, nothing else was to be expected. 'We, being men, felt our way downstairs in the dark.'

Mr Giles had risen from his seat and taken two steps with his eyes shut, to accompany his description with action, when he jumped violently, together with the rest of the company, and hurried back to his chair. The cook and housemaid screamed.

'It was a knock,' said Mr Giles, pretending to be perfectly calm. 'Open the door, somebody.'

Nobody moved.

'It seems a strange sort of thing, a knock coming at such a time in the morning,' said Mr Giles, 'but the door must be opened. Do you hear, somebody?'

Mr Giles, as he spoke, looked at Brittles, but that young man clearly considered himself to be nobody, and so he gave no reply. Mr Giles looked appealingly at the tinker, but he had suddenly fallen asleep. The women were out of the question.

'If Brittles would rather open the door in the presence of witnesses,' said Mr Giles after a short silence, 'I am ready to be one.'

'So am I,' said the tinker, waking up as suddenly as he had fallen asleep.

Brittles agreed to open the door on these terms, and they made their way upstairs with the dogs in front. The two women, who were afraid to stay below, followed behind them. On the advice of Mr Giles, they all talked very loudly, to warn anyone outside that they were strong in numbers. Mr Giles also made them pull the dogs' tails in the hall, to make them growl aggressively.

When these preparations had been made, Mr Giles gave the word of command to open the door. Brittles obeyed and the group, looking fearfully over each other's shoulders, saw no more terrifying object than poor little Oliver Twist, speechless and very, very tired, who raised his heavy eyes and silently begged for their pity.

'A boy!' cried Mr Giles, bravely pushing the tinker into the background and dragging Oliver into the hall. Then he called out, in a state of great excitement: 'Here he is! Here's one of the thieves, madam! Here's a thief, madam! Wounded, madam! I shot him, madam!'

The two women servants ran upstairs with the news that Mr Giles had captured a robber; and the tinker busied himself in trying to restore Oliver in case he should die before he could be hanged. In the middle of all this noise there was heard a sweet female voice.

'Giles!' whispered the voice from the head of the stairs.

'I'm here, miss,' replied Mr Giles. 'Don't be frightened, miss, I'm not badly injured. He didn't struggle very hard, miss.'

'Quietly!' replied the young lady. 'You are frightening my aunt as much as the thieves did. Is the poor creature seriously hurt?'

'He's badly wounded, miss,' replied Giles.

'He looks as if he is dying, miss,' called out Brittles, loudly. 'Wouldn't you like to come and look at him, miss, in case he dies?'

'Quietly!' said the lady again. 'Wait a minute or two, while I speak to Aunt.'

The speaker walked softly away and soon returned and ordered that the wounded person was to be carried carefully upstairs to Mr Giles's room, and that Brittles was to go at once to Chertsey and fetch a policeman and a doctor.

'But won't you take one look at him first, miss?' asked Mr Giles, with as much pride as if Oliver were some rare bird he had shot down.

'Not now, Giles,' replied the young lady. 'Poor fellow! Oh, treat him kindly, Giles, for my sake!'

The old servant looked up at the young lady as she turned away, with a glance as proud and admiring as if she were his own child. Then, bending over Oliver, he helped to carry him upstairs with the care and gentleness of a woman.

◆

Fagin, Charley Bates and the Dodger were playing cards when the Dodger cried: 'Listen! I heard the bell!' and, seizing up the light, walked softly upstairs.

The bell was rung again, with some impatience, while the card party remained in darkness. After a short pause, the Dodger reappeared and whispered something to Fagin.

'What!' cried the old Jew. 'Alone?'

The Dodger nodded and let in Toby Crackit.

'How are you, Fagin?' said Toby and then, pulling a chair close to the fire, he sat down. 'Don't look at me in that way, man. All in good time. I can't talk about business till I've eaten and drunk, for I haven't had a good meal for the past three days.'

Fagin motioned to the Dodger to place what food there was on the table and, seating himself opposite the housebreaker, waited to listen to what he had to say.

Toby was in no hurry to open the conversation. He ate in complete silence until he could eat no more; then, ordering Charley Bates and the Dodger out, he closed the door, mixed a glass of spirits and water and said:

'First of all, Fagin, how's Bill?'

'What!' screamed Fagin, jumping up from his seat.

'You don't mean to say −?' began Toby, turning pale.

'What?' cried Fagin, stamping on the ground in his anger. 'Where are they? Sikes and the boy! Where are they? Where have they been? Where are they hiding? Why have they not been here?'

'The attempt failed,' said Toby faintly.

'I know it,' replied the old man, taking a newspaper out of his pocket and pointing to it. 'What else?'

'They fired and hit the boy. We cut across the fields at the back, with him between us. They gave chase. The whole countryside was awake, and the dogs after us.'

'The boy!'

'Bill ran with him on his back. We stopped to take him between us; his head hung down, and he was cold. They were close on our heels; every man for himself, to save his own neck! We parted company and left the boy lying on the ground, alive or dead I don't know.'

Fagin stopped to hear no more; screaming loudly and pulling at his hair with his hands, he rushed from the room and out of the house.

Chapter 15 A Mysterious Character Appears on the Scene

Fagin had arrived at the street corner before he began to recover from the effect of Toby Crackit's information. Avoiding, as much as possible, all the main streets, he eventually came to a public bar which was the favourite meeting place of thieves and criminals.

He walked straight upstairs, and, opening the door of a room, looked anxiously about, shading his eyes with his hand, as if in search of some particular person. The room was lit by two gas-lamps, but the place was so full of tobacco smoke that at first it was hardly possible to see anything. Gradually, however, as the eye grew more used to the scene, the observer became aware of the presence of a large group of people, male and female, crowded round a long table, drinking and singing noisily.

Fagin looked eagerly from face to face, but apparently without finding the one that he was searching for. At last, catching the eye of the landlord, he made a slight signal to him and left the room.

'What can I do for you, Mr Fagin?' inquired the man, as he followed him out into the hall. 'Won't you join us?'

The old man shook his head impatiently, and said in a whisper, 'Is he here?'

'Monks, do you mean?' inquired the landlord, pausing for a moment.

'Ssh!' said Fagin. 'Yes.'

'No,' said the man, 'but I'm expecting him. If you'll wait ten minutes, he'll be here.'

'No, no,' said Fagin. 'Tell him I came here to see him and that he must come to me tonight.'

So saying, the old Jew left the place and turned his face in the direction of home. It was only an hour before midnight; the weather was unpleasantly cold, and a sharp wind was blowing. He had reached the corner of his own street when a dark figure emerged from the darkness and, crossing the road, came up to him unnoticed.

'Fagin!' whispered a voice close to his ear.

'Ah!' said the old man, turning quickly round. 'Is that –?'

'Yes!' interrupted the stranger. 'I have been waiting here for over two hours. Where the devil have you been?'

'Looking for you. On your business all night.'

'Oh, of course!' said the stranger, with a twisted smile. 'Well, and what's come of it?'

'Nothing good,' said Fagin.

They went inside together, and talked for some time in whispers. Then Monks, for this was the stranger's name, said, raising his voice a little: 'I tell you again, it was badly planned. Why did you not keep him here with the others and make a pickpocket of him from the start? Haven't you done it with other boys dozens of times? If you had had a little more patience, couldn't you have got him arrested and sent safely out of the country, perhaps for life?'

'Who would that have served, my dear?' inquired Fagin.

'Me,' replied Monks.

'But not me,' replied Fagin. 'He might have become of use to me. When there are two parties to an agreement, it is only reasonable that the interests of both should be consulted. I saw it was not easy to train him to the business; he was not like other boys in the same situation.'

59

'If he had been,' the man complained, 'he would have been a thief long ago.'

'I had no hold over him to make him worse,' continued Fagin. 'I had nothing to frighten him with. What could I do? Send him out with the Dodger and Charley? We had enough of that in the beginning, my dear; I trembled for us all.'

'That was not my fault,' remarked Monks.

'No, no, my dear,' replied Fagin. 'And I am not quarrelling with it now; because if it had never happened, you might never have seen the boy you were looking for. Well! I got him back for you by means of the girl; and then *she* begins to favour him.'

'Kill the girl,' said Monks, impatiently.

'Now, we can't afford to do that just now, my dear,' replied Fagin, smiling. 'And besides, that sort of thing is no problem to us; or, one of these days, I might be glad to have done it. I know what these girls are, Monks. As soon as the boy begins to harden, she'll care no more for him than for a block of wood. You want him made a thief. If he is alive, I can make him one, but if the worst comes to the worst and he is dead –'

'It's no fault of mine if he is!' interrupted the other man, with a look of terror, and seizing the old man's arm with trembling hands. 'Remember that, Fagin! I had no hand in it. Anything but his death, I told you from the start. I won't take blood; it's always found out, and a man has to live with it too. If they shot him dead, I was not the cause, do you hear me? Oh! What's that?'

'What?' cried Fagin, jumping to his feet. 'Where?'

'There!' replied the man, staring at the opposite wall. 'The shadow! I saw the shadow of a woman pass along the wall!'

They both rushed out of the room. There was nothing but the empty staircase. They listened for a while, but heard only a deep silence throughout the house.

'It's your imagination,' said Fagin, turning to his companion.

'I'll swear I saw a shadow,' replied Monks trembling. 'It was bending forward when I saw it first; and when I spoke, it ran away.'

Fagin looked contemptuously at the other man's pale face, and told him he could accompany him upstairs if he wished. They looked into the rooms, which were cold and empty. They went down into the passage, and from there into the cellars below: all was empty and still as death.

Chapter 16   The Kind-Hearted Dr Losberne

Two ladies were sitting at the breakfast table in a comfortable, attractive dining room. Mr Giles, dressed neatly in a black suit, was serving them. Of the two ladies, one was advanced in years but sat upright in her chair with her hands folded on the table in front of her. Her eyes were fixed on her young companion.

The young lady was not more than seventeen; she had such a slight and delicate form, she was so pure and beautiful, that earth seemed not to be her element, nor its rough creatures her fit companions.

'And Brittles has been gone more than an hour, has he?' asked the old lady, after a pause.

'An hour and twelve minutes, madam,' replied Mr Giles, consulting a silver watch which he pulled from a top pocket. At this moment a carriage drove up to the garden gate, out of which there jumped a fat gentleman who ran straight up to the door and, bursting into the room, nearly knocked over both Mr Giles and the breakfast table.

'I never heard of such a thing!' cried the fat gentleman. 'My dear Mrs Maylie – my goodness me – in the silence of the night, too – I *never* heard of such a thing!'

With these remarks, the fat gentleman shook hands with both ladies and, pulling up a chair, inquired about their health.

'Why didn't you send for me? My assistant would have come in a minute; and so would I. Dear, dear! So unexpected! In the silence of night, too!'

The doctor seemed especially troubled by the fact that the robbery had been unexpected, and attempted in the night-time; as if it were the custom of robbers to do their business in the middle of the day, and to make an appointment, by post, a day or two in advance.

'And you, Miss Rose,' said the doctor, 'I hope –'

'Oh! very much so, indeed,' said Rose, interrupting. 'But there is a poor creature upstairs, whom Aunt wishes you to see.'

'Ah! to be sure,' replied the doctor, 'so there is.' Then, turning to Giles, he asked him to show him the way.

Talking all the way, he followed Mr Giles upstairs, and while he is going upstairs the reader may be informed that the doctor was called Mr Losberne, and that he was as kind and cheerful as any doctor living.

The doctor remained a long time upstairs. A large box was fetched out of the carriage, and a bedroom bell was rung often. Finally he returned to the ladies, looking very mysterious.

'This is a very extraordinary thing, Mrs Maylie,' said the doctor.

'He is not in danger, I hope?' said the old lady.

'I don't think he is,' replied the doctor. 'Have you seen the thief?'

'No,' replied the old lady.

'Nor heard anything about him?'

'No.'

'I beg your pardon, madam,' interrupted Mr Giles; 'but I was going to tell you about him when Dr Losberne came in.'

The fact was that Mr Giles had received such praise for his courage that he could not help delaying the explanation for a few happy moments.

'Rose wished to see the man,' said Mrs Maylie, 'but I wouldn't hear of it.'

'There is nothing very alarming in his appearance,' replied the doctor. 'Have you any objection to seeing him in my presence?'

'If it is necessary,' replied the old lady, 'certainly not.'

'I think it is necessary,' said the doctor. 'Anyway, I am quite sure that you would deeply regret it if you did not. He is perfectly quiet and comfortable now. I would like you both to come and see him.'

He led the way upstairs to Giles's room where, instead of the evil-faced criminal they expected to see, there lay a child upon the bed; a mere child, worn with pain and sunk into a deep sleep. His injured arm lay across his chest, and his head leaned on the other arm.

The doctor watched the patient while the younger lady seated herself in a chair by the bedside. As she bent over the child, her tears fell upon his forehead. The boy smiled in his sleep, as if these marks of pity had allowed him to dream of the love and affection he had never known.

'What can this mean?' cried the older lady. 'This poor child can never have been the pupil of robbers!'

'My dear lady,' said the doctor, sadly shaking his head, 'crime, like death, is not restricted to the old and ugly alone. The youngest and fairest are too often its chosen victims.'

'But can you really believe that this delicate boy has been the voluntary partner of criminals?' asked Rose.

The doctor shook his head, as if to say that he feared it was very possible; and, observing that they might wake the patient, led the way into another room.

'But even if he has behaved badly,' continued Rose, 'think how young he is, think that he may never have known a mother's love or the comfort of a home; that ill-treatment may have driven him into the company of men who have forced him to lead a life of crime. Aunt, dear Aunt, think of this before you let them drag him to a prison. Oh! As you love me, who might have been helpless and unprotected but for your goodness and affection, have pity upon him before it is too late!'

'My dear love,' said the older lady, 'do you think I would harm a hair of his head? No, surely. My days are drawing to their close; and may pity be shown to me as I show it to others! What can I do to save him, sir?'

'Let me think, madam,' said the doctor. 'Let me think.' Dr Losberne pushed his hands into his pockets and walked up and down the room several times, often stopping and balancing himself on his toes or crying 'I've got it now' or 'No, I haven't'. In the end he came to a stop without finding any resolution to the problem.

Hour after hour passed, and still Oliver slept heavily. It was evening, indeed, before the kind-hearted doctor brought them the news that the boy was sufficiently recovered to be spoken to.

Oliver told them all his simple history, and was often forced by pain or weakness to pause before continuing. After the sick child had told of the many evils and misfortunes which cruel men had brought him, though, beauty and virtue watched him as he slept.

Dr Losberne went down to the kitchen to talk to Mr Giles.

'How is the patient tonight, sir?' asked Giles.

'Reasonably well,' replied the doctor. 'I am afraid you have got yourself into trouble there, Mr Giles.'

'I hope you don't mean to say, sir,' said Mr Giles, trembling, 'that he's going to die. If I thought it, I should never be happy again.'

'That's not the point,' said the doctor mysteriously. 'The point is this: are you ready to swear, you and Brittles here, that that boy upstairs is the boy that was put through the little window last night? Out with it!'

The doctor made this demand in such a strong tone of

pretended anger that Giles and Brittles stared at each other in confusion.

'Here's a house broken into,' said the doctor, 'and a couple of men catch one moment's sight of a boy, in the middle of gunpowder smoke and in all the confusion of alarm and darkness. Here's a boy who comes to that same house, the next morning and, because he happens to have an injured arm, these men lay violent hands upon him – by doing which they put his life in great danger and swear he is the thief. Now, the question is, whether these men are justified in so doing. I ask you again, Giles and Brittles, do you swear that you are able to identify that boy?'

Brittles looked doubtfully at Mr Giles; Mr Giles looked doubtfully at Brittles; the two women and the tinker leaned forward to listen. At that moment a ring was heard at the gate, and at the same moment the sound of wheels. It was the police officers who had been sent for.

Dr Losberne led them upstairs to Oliver's bedroom. Oliver had been sleeping, but he was still feverish. With the assistance of the doctor, he managed to sit up in bed for a minute or so and looked at the strangers without at all understanding what was going on.

'This,' said Dr Losberne, 'is the lad who, after being accidentally wounded by a gun, comes to the house for assistance this morning and is arrested and ill-treated by that gentleman with the candle in his hand.'

Mr Giles was in a state of considerable fear and amazement. The police officers questioned him. All he could say at first was that he *thought* the boy was the housebreakers' boy; then, on being further questioned, he said he didn't know what to think; in the end he said that he was almost certain it wasn't the same boy.

In short, after some more questions, and a great deal more conversation, the police officers were convinced that Giles had made a stupid mistake and that Oliver had nothing to do with the housebreakers. Both policemen returned to town, and Oliver was left to the loving care of Mrs Maylie, Rose and the kind-hearted Dr Losberne.

Chapter 17   Oliver's Life with the Maylies

Oliver's sufferings were neither slight nor few. In addition to the pain from his wounded arm, his exposure to the wet and cold had brought on fever which hung around him for many weeks and made him extremely weak. But in the end he began to get slowly better and was able to say, in a few tearful words, how deeply he felt the goodness of the two sweet ladies, and how sincerely he hoped that when he grew strong and well again he could do something to show them how grateful he was.

'Poor fellow!' said Rose, when Oliver had been trying one day to thank her. 'You shall have many opportunities of serving us, if you would like to. We are going into the country, and my aunt is planning to take you with us. The quiet place, the pure air, and all the pleasures and beauties of spring will restore your health in a few days. We will employ you in a hundred ways, when you are strong enough.'

'Oh!' cried Oliver. 'I would be so happy to work for you!'

'You shall,' said Rose.

A fortnight later, when the fine warm weather had really begun and every tree and flower was putting out its young leaves and rich flowers, they made preparations for leaving the house at Chertsey for some months. Leaving Giles and another servant in charge of the house, they moved to a cottage in the country, and took Oliver with them.

Oliver, whose past had been full of noise and quarrelling, seemed to start a new life in this lovely spot. The days were peaceful and calm; the nights brought no fear. Every morning he went to an old gentleman who lived near the little village church, who taught him to read better and to write. Then he would walk with Mrs Maylie and Rose, and hear them talk about books; or perhaps sit near them in some shady place, and listen while the young lady read. Then he had his own lesson to prepare for the next day. In the evening there were more walks, and at night the young lady would sit down at the piano and play some pleasant tune, or sing in a low gentle voice some old song which it pleased her aunt to hear.

So three months passed; three months of perfect happiness. With the purest and kindest generosity on the one side, and the warmest appreciation on the other, it is no wonder that, by the end of that short time, Oliver Twist had become a strongly attached and dearly loved member of the small family.

Chapter 18   The Mysterious Character Reappears

Mr Bumble, who was now a married man and master of the workhouse, feeling unhappy one day after a little family quarrel with Mrs Bumble, left the workhouse and walked around the streets. Desiring a drink, he paused before a public house whose sitting room, as he gathered from a quick glance through the window, was deserted except for one single customer. It began to rain heavily at that moment. This determined him; he stepped in and, ordering something to drink as he passed the bar, entered the room into which he had looked from the street.

The man who was seated there was tall and dark, and wore a heavy coat. He had the air of a stranger, and seemed by the dustiness of his clothes to have travelled some distance. He eyed Bumble sideways as he entered, but hardly answered his greeting. Mr Bumble drank in silence, and read the paper with an air of importance.

It happened, however, that Mr Bumble felt, every now and then, a strong desire to steal a look at the stranger. Whenever he did so, he found that the stranger was at the same moment stealing a look at him.

When their eyes had met several times in this way, the stranger said in a deep voice: 'Were you looking for me when you looked in at the window?'

'Not that I am aware of, unless you're Mr –' Here Mr Bumble stopped short, for he wanted to know the stranger's name, and thought that he might supply it.

'I see you were not,' said the stranger, 'or you would have known my name. But I know you pretty well. What are you now?'

'Master of the workhouse,' answered Mr Bumble, slowly and impressively.

'You have the same sense of self-interest that you always had, I doubt not?' continued the stranger, looking keenly into Mr Bumble's eyes, as the latter looked at him in surprise at the question.

'I suppose a married man,' replied Mr Bumble, 'has no more objection to earning an honest penny than a single man. Workhouse masters are not so well paid that they can afford to refuse any little extra money when it comes to them in the proper manner.'

The stranger smiled and nodded his head, as if to say he was not wrong about Mr Bumble; then he rang the bell.

'Fill this glass again,' he said, handing Mr Bumble's empty glass to the landlord. 'Let it be strong. You like it so, I suppose?'

'Not too strong,' replied Mr Bumble, with a delicate cough.

The landlord smiled, disappeared, and shortly afterwards returned with a steaming glass, of which the first mouthful brought tears into Mr Bumble's eyes.

'Now listen to me,' said the stranger, after closing the door and window. 'I came down to this place today to find you. I want some information from you. I don't ask you to give it for nothing, slight as it is.'

As he spoke, he pushed a couple of gold pounds across the table to his companion. When Mr Bumble had carefully examined the coins to see that they were real gold, and put them in his pocket, the stranger went on: 'Carry your memory back – let me see – twelve years last winter.'

'It's a long time,' said Mr Bumble. 'Very good. I've done it.'

'The scene, the workhouse.'

'Good!'

'And the time, night.'

'Yes.'

'And the place, the room where poor women gave birth to children for the parish to bring them up before they hid their shame in the grave! A boy was born there.'

'Many boys,' agreed Mr Bumble.

'I speak of one in particular; a gentle-looking boy, who was apprenticed down here to a coffin-maker – I wish he had made his coffin, and was then buried in it – and who afterwards ran away to London.'

'Why, you mean Oliver! Young Twist!' said Mr Bumble. 'I remember him, of course. There wasn't a more strong-willed young villain –'

'It's not of him I want to hear,' said the stranger, 'it's of a woman, the old woman who nursed his mother. Where is she?'

'She died last winter,' answered Mr Bumble.

The man stared at him when he had given this information. For some time, he appeared doubtful whether he ought to be happy or disappointed at the information; but in the end he remarked that it did not matter much, and rose to leave.

But Mr Bumble saw at once that an opportunity was opened for him to make some money. He remembered that his wife, who had been a nurse in the workhouse before he married her, was in possession of a secret relating to that old woman. He informed the stranger that one woman had been alone with the old nurse shortly before she died; and that she could throw some light on the subject of his inquiry.

'How can I find her?' said the stranger, thrown off his guard, and plainly showing that this information frightened him again.

'Only through me,' replied Mr Bumble.

'When?' cried the stranger quickly.

'Tomorrow,' replied Mr Bumble.

'At nine in the evening,' said the stranger, producing a piece of paper and writing down an address by the waterside. 'Bring her to me there. I needn't tell you to keep this a secret. It's in your own interest.'

With these words he paid for the drinks and left.

On looking at the address, Mr Bumble observed that it contained no name. He ran after the stranger and said: 'What name shall I ask for?'

'Monks!' replied the man, and walked rapidly away.

Chapter 19   A Meeting at Night

It was a dull, rainy summer evening when Mr and Mrs Bumble, turning out of the main street of the town, headed towards a group of ruined houses about a mile and a half away from it, built on low, unhealthy wet land bordering on the river.

In the heart of this group of buildings stood a larger building once used as a factory of some kind but long since gone to ruin. It was in front of this decayed building that Mr and Mrs Bumble stopped. 'The place should be somewhere here,' said Bumble, consulting a piece of paper he held in his hand.

'Hullo there!' cried a voice from above. 'Stand still a minute.

I'll be with you immediately.'

Soon a small door opened and Monks waved them inside.

'Come in!' he cried impatiently. 'Don't keep me waiting here!'

The woman, who had at first seemed uncertain, walked in, followed rather unwillingly by Mr Bumble. Monks led the way up a ladder to another floor above and quickly closed the door of the room in which they were. Then he lowered a lamp which hung at the end of a rope and which cast a small amount of light on an old table and three chairs that were placed beneath it.

'Now,' said Monks, when they had all three seated themselves, 'the sooner we come to our business the better for all. The woman knows what it is, does she?'

Mrs Bumble said that she was perfectly familiar with it.

'He is right in saying that you were with this old nurse the night she died, and that she told you something –'

'About the mother of the boy you named,' replied Mrs Bumble, interrupting him. 'Yes.'

'The first question is, what was the subject of her information?' said Monks.

'That's the second,' observed the woman with much determination. 'The first is, what may the information be worth?'

'Who the devil can tell that, without knowing what kind of information it is?' asked Monks.

'Nobody better than you, I am sure,' answered Mrs Bumble.

'How much do you want?' asked Monks crossly.

'What's it worth to you?' asked the woman coolly.

'It may be nothing; it may be twenty pounds,' replied Monks. 'Speak out, and let me know which.'

'Add five pounds to the sum you have named; give me five-and-twenty pounds in gold,' said the woman, 'and I'll tell you all I know. Not before.'

'What if I pay it for nothing?' asked Monks.

'You can easily take it away again,' replied the woman. 'I am

71

just a woman, alone here and unprotected.'

'Not alone, my dear, nor unprotected either,' said Mr Bumble, in a voice trembling with fear. 'I am here, my dear.'

'You are a fool,' said Mrs Bumble in reply, 'and had better hold your tongue.'

Mr Monks put his hand into a side-pocket and counted out twenty-five gold pounds on the table. He pushed them over to the woman.

'Now,' he said, 'gather them up, and let's hear your story.'

'When this woman, the woman we called Old Sally, died,' Mrs Bumble began, 'she and I were alone. She spoke of a young woman who had brought a child into the world some years before. The child was the one you named to him last night,' said the woman, nodding carelessly towards her husband. 'The mother was robbed by the nurse.'

'In life?' asked Monks.

'In death,' replied Mrs Bumble. 'She stole from the dead body something which the dead woman had begged her, with her last breath, to keep for the child.'

'She sold it?' cried Monks desperately. 'Did she sell it? Where? When? To whom? How long ago?'

'As she told me, with great difficulty, that she had done this,' said the woman, 'she fell back and died.'

'Without saying more?' cried Monks angrily. 'It's a lie! I'll not be played with. She said more. I'll kill you both, but I'll know what it was.'

'She didn't say another word,' said the woman, unmoved by the strange man's violence, 'but she pulled my dress violently with one hand, which was partly closed; and when I saw that she was dead and removed the hand by force, I found that it held a bit of jewellery.'

'Where is it now?' asked Monks quickly.

'There,' replied the woman, and she threw on the table a small leather bag which Monks opened with trembling hands. It contained a gold chain, two locks of hair, and a plain gold wedding ring.

'And is this all?' said Monks, after carefully examining the contents of the little packet.

'All,' replied the woman. 'Is that what you expected to get from me?'

'It is,' replied Monks.

'What do you propose to do with it? Can it be used against me?'

'Never,' replied Monks. 'Nor against me either. See here! But don't move a step forward, or your life will be worth nothing.'

With these words he suddenly pushed the table aside, and, pulling an iron ring in the boards of the floor, threw back a large door which opened at Mr Bumble's feet, and caused that gentleman to take several rapid steps backward.

'Look down,' said Monks, lowering the lamp through the opening. 'Don't fear me. I could have let you fall down there when you were seated over it, if that had been my intention.'

Thus encouraged, Mr and Mrs Bumble drew near to the edge of the opening; the muddy water, swollen by the heavy rain, was rushing past below.

Monks took the little packet from his pocket and, tying it to a piece of lead, dropped it into the stream. It fell straight into the water and was gone.

The three looking into each other's faces seemed to breathe more freely.

'There!' said Monks, closing the door. 'Light your lamp, and get away from here as fast as you can.'

Mr Bumble lit his lamp and climbed the ladder in silence, followed by his wife, with Monks behind her.

They crossed the lower room slowly and carefully, for Monks jumped at every shadow; and Mr Bumble, holding his lamp a foot above the ground, looked nervously around him for hidden openings. The gate through which they had entered was softly unlocked and opened by Monks, and the couple emerged into the wet and darkness outside.

Chapter 20   Bill Sikes Is Ill

On the next evening Bill Sikes, waking from a short sleep, angrily asked what time of night it was.

'Not long after seven,' said Nancy. 'How do you feel tonight, Bill?'

'As weak as water,' replied Mr Sikes. 'Here, lend me a hand and help me to get off this bed.'

Illness had not improved Mr Sikes's temper; as the girl raised him up and led him to a chair, he swore at her awkwardness and hit her.

The room in which they were was not the one they had lived in before the attempted robbery at Chertsey, although it was in the same part of the town. It was a small room with little furniture, off a narrow, dirty lane. It was evident that they now lived in a state of extreme poverty.

'Don't be too hard on me tonight, Bill,' said the girl, putting her hand upon his shoulder.

'Why not?' cried Sikes.

'So many nights,' said the girl, with a touch of womanly affection, 'I have been nursing and caring for you, as if you were a child. And this is the first night that I've seen you better and like yourself. You wouldn't have treated me as you did just now if you'd thought of that, would you? Come, come; say you wouldn't.'

'Well, then,' replied Mr Sikes, 'I wouldn't. But don't stand crying there. You won't affect me with your woman's nonsense.'

At that moment Fagin appeared at the door, followed by the Artful Dodger and Charley Bates.

'Why, what evil wind has blown you here?' said Mr Sikes to Fagin.

'Ah!' said Fagin, rubbing his hands with great satisfaction. 'You're better, Bill, I can see.'

'Better!' exclaimed Mr Sikes. 'I might have been dead twenty times over before you'd have done anything to help me. What do you mean by leaving a man in this state three weeks and more, you false-hearted villain? If it hadn't been for the girl I might have died.'

'There now, Bill,' said Fagin, eagerly catching at the word. 'If it hadn't been for the girl! Who but poor old Fagin was the means of your having such a useful girl around you?'

'That's true enough!' said Nancy.

'Oh, well,' said Mr Sikes to Fagin, 'but I must have some money from you tonight.'

'I haven't a single coin on me,' replied the old man.

'But you've got lots at home,' said Sikes, 'and I must have some from there.'

'Lots!' cried Fagin, holding up his hands. 'I haven't enough to—'

'I don't know how much you've got,' interrupted Sikes. 'But I must have some tonight.'

'Well, well,' said Fagin. 'I'll send the Artful soon.'

'You won't do anything of the kind,' replied Mr Sikes. 'Nancy will go and get it; and I'll have a short sleep while she's gone.'

Fagin then left Sikes and returned home accompanied by Nancy and the boys.

When they arrived at his house, Fagin sent the boys away from the room and then said to Nancy: 'I'll go and get you that money, Nancy. This is only the key of a little cupboard where I keep a few odd things the boys collect, my dear. I never lock up my money, for I've got none to lock up, my dear. It's a poor trade,

Nancy; and there are no thanks from anyone. But I'm fond of seeing the young people around me, and I bear it all, I bear it all. Ssh!' he said suddenly, hiding the key under his coat. 'Who's that? Listen!'

The visitor, hurrying into the room, was close to the girl before he noticed her.

It was Monks.

'Only one of my young people,' said Fagin, observing that Monks drew back on seeing a stranger. Then pointing upstairs, he took Monks out of the room.

Before the sound of their footsteps had ceased to ring out through the house, the girl had slipped off her shoes; then she softly climbed the stairs and was lost in the darkness above.

The room remained deserted for a quarter of an hour or more; then the girl hurried back down, and immediately afterwards the two men were heard returning. Monks went at once into the street, and Fagin went upstairs again for the money. When he came back, the girl was preparing to go.

'Why, Nance,' remarked Fagin, staring at her as he put down the candle, 'how pale you are!'

With a feeling of regret for every piece of money lost to him, he counted the amount into her hand and they parted without more conversation. When the girl got into the open street, she sat down on a doorstep and seemed, for a few moments, unable to continue her journey. Suddenly she stood up and, hurrying on, soon reached home.

Sikes did not notice her state of anxiety. He merely inquired if she had brought the money and, receiving a satisfactory reply, returned to the sleep which her arrival had interrupted.

Chapter 21   Nancy Pays a Secret Visit

The next day Sikes was too occupied, eating and drinking with the money the girl had brought, to notice anything unusual in her behaviour. But as that day ended, the girl's excitement increased, and when night came and she sat waiting for him to drink himself to sleep, there was an unusual paleness in her cheek and a fire in her eye that even Sikes observed with surprise.

'Why!' said the man, raising himself on his hands as he stared the girl in the face. 'You look like a dead body come to life. What's the matter?'

'Matter?' replied the girl. 'Nothing. What are you staring at me for?'

'What is it?' demanded Sikes, seizing her arm and shaking her roughly. 'What are you thinking about?'

'About many things, Bill,' replied the girl, trembling.

'You've caught the fever,' said Sikes. 'Come and sit beside me and put your own face on again or I'll alter it so that you won't recognize it.'

The girl obeyed. Sikes, holding her hand in his, fell back on the bed, turning his eyes towards her face. They closed, opened again, then closed once more. He fell at last into a deep sleep.

'The drug has finally taken effect,' whispered the girl as she rose from the bedside. 'I may be too late even now.'

She quickly put on her hat and coat, looking fearfully round from time to time as if she expected at any minute to feel the pressure of Sikes's heavy hand upon her shoulder. Then, bending softly over the bed, she kissed his lips, and noiselessly left the house.

Many of the shops were already closing in the back lanes through which she walked on her way to the West End of London. The clock struck ten, increasing her impatience. She ran along the narrow streets, pushing past people who stood in her way. When she reached the more wealthy part of the town, the streets were much emptier. At last she reached a family hotel in a quiet but attractive street near Hyde Park. After standing for a few seconds as though making up her mind, she entered the hall.

'Now, young woman!' said a smartly dressed maid. 'Who do you want here?'

'Miss Maylie,' said Nancy.

The young woman, who had by this time noted her appearance, called a man to answer her.

'Come,' said the man, pushing her towards the door. 'None of this! Out you go.'

'You will have to carry me out,' said the girl violently. 'Isn't there anybody here that will carry a simple message from a poor girl like me?'

'What is it to be?' said the man, softened at last.

'That a young woman asks to speak to Miss Maylie alone,' said Nancy. 'And that if the lady will only hear the first word she has to say, she will know whether to hear her or turn her out of doors.'

The man ran upstairs and soon returned and told the woman to follow him. With trembling legs she followed him to a small room, where he left her to wait.

◆

The girl's life had been wasted in the streets, but there was something of woman's original nature in her still. When she heard a light step approaching and thought of the wide contrast which the small room would in another moment contain, she felt burdened with the sense of her own deep shame.

She raised her eyes sufficiently to observe that the figure which presented itself was that of a slight and beautiful girl.

'I am the person you inquired for,' said the young lady in a sweet voice. 'Tell me why you wished to see me.'

78

The kind tone, the sweet voice, the gentle manner, took the girl completely by surprise, and she burst into tears.

'Oh, lady, lady!' cried the girl. 'If there were more like you, there would be fewer like me.'

'Sit down,' said Rose. 'If you are in poverty or trouble, I shall be truly glad to help you if I can. Sit down.'

'Let me stand, lady,' said the girl, still crying, 'and do not speak to me so kindly till you know me better. Is that door shut?'

'Yes,' said Rose. 'Why?'

'Because,' said the girl, 'I am about to put my life, and the lives of others, in your hands. I am the girl that dragged little Oliver back to old Fagin's on the night he went out from the house in Pentonville.'

'You!' said Rose Maylie.

'I, lady!' replied the girl. 'I am the terrible creature you have heard of, that lives among thieves and that has never known any better life. Do not mind showing your dislike of me openly. The poorest women fall back as I make my way along a crowded street.'

'What things you are saying!' said Rose.

'Thank heaven, dear lady,' cried the girl, 'that you had friends to care for you in your childhood, and that you were never in the middle of cold and hunger and drunkenness as I have been from my earliest days.'

'I pity you!' said Rose, with real sympathy. 'It breaks my heart to hear you!'

'Heaven reward you for your goodness!' said the girl. 'I have escaped from those who would surely murder me, if they knew I had been here, to tell you what I have heard. Do you know a man called Monks?'

'No,' said Rose. 'I never heard the name.'

'He knows you,' replied the girl, 'and knew you were here, for it was by hearing him speak about the place that I found out where you are. Some time ago, and soon after Oliver was put into your house on the night of the robbery, I heard a conversation between this man and Fagin in the dark. I found out that Monks had seen Oliver accidentally with two of our boys on the day we first lost him and had known immediately that he was the same child that he was watching for, though I couldn't understand why. Monks promised Fagin a large sum of money if Oliver was brought back; and he was to have more for making Oliver a thief.'

'For what purpose?' asked Rose.

'I couldn't find out; I had to escape discovery, for he had caught sight of my shadow on the wall as I listened. I saw him no more till last night.'

'And what happened then?'

'I'll tell you, lady. Last night he came again and again I listened at the door. I heard Monks say: "So the only proof of the boy's identity lies at the bottom of the river, and the old woman that received these things from his mother will never leave her coffin." '

'What is all this?' said Rose.

'The truth, lady, though it comes from my lips,' replied the girl. 'Then he said that if he could take the boy's life without risking his own neck, he would; but as he couldn't, he'd continue to find him at every turn in life and to harm him. "In short, Fagin," he says, "Even *you* never laid such traps as I'll lay for my young brother, Oliver." '

'His brother!' cried Rose.

'Those were his words,' said Nancy, glancing anxiously around, unable to forget for a moment about Sikes. 'And now it is growing late, and I must go.'

'But what can I do?' said Rose. 'To what use can I put this information? Why do you wish to return to companions you paint in such terrible colours? If you repeat this information to a gentleman whom I know, you can be put in some place of safety without delay.'

'I wish to go back,' said the girl. 'I must go back because – how can I tell such things to a lady like you – because among the men I have told you of, there is one I can't leave; no, not even to be saved from the life I am leading now.'

'Oh!' said the girl. 'Do not turn a deaf ear to my request. Do hear my words and let me save you.'

'Lady,' cried the girl, sinking on her knees, 'you are the first that ever spoke such words to me, and if I had heard them years ago, they might have turned me from a life of sin and sorrow; but it is too late!'

'It is never too late,' argued Rose.

'It is,' cried the girl. 'I cannot leave him now! I could not be the cause of his death. If I told others what I have told you, he would be sure to die. I must go back. Something draws me back to him in spite of all my suffering and his cruelty and ill-treatment.'

'What am I to do?' said Rose. 'How can we save Oliver?'

'You must know some kind gentleman that will advise you what to do,' answered the girl.

'But where can I find you again when it is necessary?'

'Will you promise me that you will keep my secret and come to meet me alone or with the only other person that knows it, and that I shall not be watched or followed?'

'I promise you faithfully,' said Rose.

'Every Sunday night, from eleven until midnight,' said the girl, 'I will walk on London Bridge if I am alive.'

'Stay another moment,' said Rose as the girl hurried towards the door. 'Will you return to this gang of robbers, and to this man, when a word can save you? I wish to serve you.'

'You would serve me best, lady,' replied the girl, 'if you could take my life at once. I have felt more grief to think of what I am, tonight, than I ever did before, and it would be something not to die in the hell in which I have lived. May God bring you as much happiness, sweet lady, as I have brought shame to myself!'

The unhappy creature turned to leave. Rose Maylie, quite overcome by this extraordinary meeting, sank into a chair and tried to collect her wandering thoughts.

Chapter 22   Mr Grimwig's Strange Behaviour

The Maylies had come to London to spend just three days before leaving for a distant part of the coast.

Rose was in a difficult situation. She was anxious to solve the mystery which surrounded Oliver's history, and yet at the same time she could not break her promise of secrecy to the poor woman who had taken her into her confidence.

She was in this restless condition the morning after Nancy's mysterious visit when Oliver came into the room in a state of breathless excitement. He told her that he had seen the gentleman who had been so good to him – Mr Brownlow – getting out of a coach. The boy was crying with pleasure as he told the story; he had found out his address.

'Look here,' said Oliver, showing her a piece of paper, 'here it is; here's where he lives. I'm going there now! Oh, dear me, dear me! What shall I do when I see him again?'

Rose read the address, which was in the Strand, and very soon decided to make use of that discovery.

'Quick!' she said. 'Tell them to fetch a carriage, and be ready to go with me. I will take you there immediately; I will only tell my aunt that we are going out for an hour, and I will be ready as soon as you are.'

In less than five minutes they were on their way to Mr Brownlow's. When they arrived there, Rose left Oliver in the coach, giving him the excuse of preparing the old gentleman to receive him; and, sending her card with a servant, requested to see Mr Brownlow on very urgent business.

The servant soon returned to beg her to walk upstairs. She followed him into an upper room and was presented to Mr Brownlow, who was sitting with his old friend, Mr Grimwig.

Rose told Mr Brownlow that he had once shown great kindness to a young boy who was a dear friend of hers and added that she was sure he would take an interest in hearing about him again.

'Indeed!' said Mr Brownlow.

'Oliver Twist, you knew him as,' replied Rose.

The words no sooner escaped her lips than Mr Grimwig, who had been reading a large book that lay on the table, upset it with a great crash and, falling back in his chair, gave a cry of great wonder. Mr Brownlow was no less surprised, although his amazement was not expressed in the same odd manner. He drew his chair near to Miss Maylie's and said: 'Do me the favour, my dear young lady, of leaving entirely out of the question that kindness of which you speak; and if you can produce any evidence which will alter the low opinion I once had of that poor child, in heaven's name let me have it.'

'A bad one! I'll eat my head if he is not a bad one,' said Mr Grimwig.

'He is a child of a noble nature and a warm heart,' said Rose, reddening, 'and he has feelings which would do honour to many people six times his age.'

'I'm only sixty-one,' said Mr Grimwig, 'and as Oliver is twelve years old at least, I don't see the sense of your remark.'

'Do not mind what he says, Miss Maylie,' said Mr Brownlow. 'He does not mean it.'

'Yes, he does,' growled Mr Grimwig.

'No, he does not,' said Mr Brownlow, his anger rising.

'He'll eat his head if he doesn't,' growled Mr Grimwig.

'He would deserve to have it knocked off, if he does,' said Mr Brownlow.

'And he'd like to see any man offer to do it,' replied Mr Grimwig, knocking his stick to the floor.

Having gone this far in their quarrel, the two gentlemen took snuff and then shook hands according to their custom.

'Now, Miss Maylie, to return to the subject in which you are so much interested. Let me know what information you have of this child.'

Rose at once told him all that had happened to Oliver since he left Mr Brownlow's house, adding that Oliver's only sorrow, for some months past, had been that he could not meet with his former helper and friend.

'Thank God!' said the old gentleman. 'This is great happiness to me, great happiness. But you haven't told me where he is now, Miss Maylie. Why haven't you brought him with you?'

'He is waiting in a coach at the door,' replied Rose.

'At this door!' cried the old gentleman, hurrying out of the room and down the stairs without another word.

When he had gone, Mr Grimwig rose from his chair and moved as fast as he could up and down the room at least a dozen times before stopping suddenly in front of Rose and kissing her.

'Ssh!' he said, as the young lady rose in some alarm at this unusual behaviour. 'Don't be afraid. I'm old enough to be your grandfather. You're a sweet girl. I like you. Here they are!'

Mr Brownlow returned, accompanied by Oliver, whom Mr Grimwig received very kindly.

'There is somebody else who should not be forgotten,' said Mr Brownlow, ringing the bell. 'Send Mrs Bedwin here, if you please.'

Oliver's old nurse came quickly and stood at the door, waiting for orders.

'Why, you get blinder every day, Bedwin,' said Mr Brownlow. 'Put on your glasses and see if you can't find out what you were wanted for.'

The old lady began to search in her pockets for her glasses. But Oliver could wait no longer: he ran into her arms.

'God be good to me!' cried the old nurse, holding him tightly. 'It is my sweet boy!'

'My dear old nurse!' cried Oliver.

'He would come back – I knew he would,' said the old woman, holding him in her arms. 'Where have you been, this long, long while? Ah! The same sweet face, but not so pale; the same soft eyes, but not so sad.'

Leaving her with Oliver, Mr Brownlow led the way into another room; there he heard from Rose a full account of her meeting with Nancy, and readily promised to consider what should be done.

Then Rose and Oliver returned home.

Chapter 23 The Artful Dodger Gets into Trouble

Fagin was at home with his pupils. But the Artful Dodger was not among them; the police had accused him of attempting to pick a pocket and, finding a silver snuff-box on him, had arrested him. Fagin was anxious about him, for the police knew what a clever fellow the Dodger was and they were sure to bring strong evidence against him. One of the boys was sent to attend the trial in order to give a full account of it to Fagin.

The Dodger came into the courtroom with the arms of his coat turned up as usual, his left hand in his pocket and his hat in his right hand. Taking his place in the dock, he requested to know 'what he was placed in that shameful situation for'.

'Hold your tongue, will you?' said his guard.

'I'm an Englishman, aren't I?' answered the Dodger. 'Where are my rights?'

'You'll get your rights soon enough,' said the guard, 'and salt and pepper with them.'

'We'll see what the Secretary of State for Home Affairs has got to say about that,' replied Mr Dawkins. 'Now then! What is this business? I hope that the magistrates won't keep me too long while they read the paper, for I've got an appointment with a gentleman in the City.★ He'll go away if I'm not there in time, and then perhaps there will be an action for damages against those who are keeping me away.'

The members of the public laughed loudly at this.

'Silence there!' cried the guard.

'What is this?' asked one of the magistrates.

'A pickpocketing case, sir.'

'Has the boy ever been here before?'

'He ought to have been, many times,' replied the guard. 'I know him pretty well, sir.'

'Oh! You know me, do you?' cried the Artful, making a note of the statement. 'Very good. That's an offence against my character.'

Here there was another laugh, and another cry of 'Silence!'

'Now then, where are the witnesses?' said the clerk.

'Ah! That's right,' added the Dodger. 'Where are they? I should like to see them.'

This wish was immediately granted, for a policeman stepped forward who had seen the prisoner pick the pocket of a gentleman, and when he was arrested and searched a silver snuff-box, with the owner's name on the lid, was found in his pocket.

'Have you anything to ask this witness, boy?' said the magistrate.

★ the City: an area of central London which is Britain's financial centre.

'No,' replied the Dodger, 'not here, for this isn't a court of justice; and besides, my lawyer is having breakfast this morning at the House of Commons. But I shall have something to say elsewhere and I'll–'

'There! Take him away,' interrupted the magistrate.

'Come on,' said his guard.

'Oh, I'll come on,' replied the Dodger, brushing his hat with his hand. 'I wouldn't go free now if you were to fall down on your knees and ask me. Here, carry me off to prison! Take me away!'

With these words the Dodger allowed himself to be led off by the collar, threatening to make parliamentary business of it.

Having seen him locked up by himself in a little cell, Fagin's boy hurried back to his master to give him the news that the Dodger was making a fine reputation for himself.

Chapter 24   Nancy Keeps Her Promise

It was Sunday night, and the bell of the nearest church struck the hour. Sikes and Fagin were talking, but they paused to listen. The girl looked up from the low seat on which she lay, and listened too. Eleven o'clock.

Nancy put on her hat and was leaving the room.

'Hullo!' cried Sikes. 'Where are you going to, Nancy, at this time of night?'

'Not far.'

'What answer's that?' returned Sikes. 'Where are you going?'

'I don't know where,' replied the girl.

'Then I do,' said Sikes. 'Nowhere. Sit down.'

'I'm not well. I told you that before,' answered the girl. 'I want a breath of air.'

'Put your head out of the window,' replied Sikes.

'There's not enough there,' said the girl. 'I want it in the street.'

'Then you won't have it,' replied Sikes, rising and locking the door. Pulling her hat from her head he threw it on the top of an old cupboard. 'Now stop quietly where you are, will you?'

'Let me go,' said the girl, kneeling on the floor. 'Bill, let me go for only one hour.'

'You're mad!' cried Sikes, seizing her roughly by the arm. 'Get up!'

'Not till you let me go – never, never!' shouted the girl. Sikes looked on, for a moment, and suddenly took both her hands and dragged her into a small room. He threw her into a chair and held her down by force. She struggled and begged by turns until twelve o'clock had struck and then she became quiet. Sikes left her to recover and returned to Fagin.

'Whew!' said Sikes, wiping his face. 'What a strange girl she is!'

'You may say that, Bill,' replied Fagin thoughtfully. 'You may say that.'

Fagin walked towards his home, thinking hard about the scene he had just witnessed. The girl's altered manner and her impatience to leave home that night at a particular hour had made him think that Nancy, tired of Sikes's cruelty, had found a new friend. Such a new friend would be valuable to him, and must be identified without delay.

Before he had reached his home, he had made his plans. He would have Nancy watched and discover the object of her new affection.

◆

A week passed: it was Sunday night again. The church clocks struck a quarter to twelve, as two figures appeared on London Bridge. One, advancing with a rapid step, was that of a woman who looked eagerly about her as though in search of some expected object. The other figure was that of a man, who followed her at some distance, walking in the deepest shadow he could find. Thus they crossed the bridge. At the other side the woman, apparently disappointed in her search, turned back. The movement was sudden, but her pursuer quickly hid himself. Near the middle of the bridge, she stopped. The man stopped too.

Two minutes later a young lady, accompanied by a grey-haired gentleman, stepped down from a carriage within a short distance of the bridge and walked straight towards it. They had hardly set foot on the bridge when the girl hurried towards them.

They gave cries of surprise when she suddenly joined them, and stopped to talk, but Nancy said quickly: 'Not here; I am afraid to speak to you here. Come away from the public road – down those steps!'

When the man who was secretly following Nancy heard these words, and saw her pointing to the steps, he hurried there unobserved and hid in a dark turning in the flight of steps. Soon he heard the sound of footsteps, and voices very close to his ear. He pulled himself straight upright against the wall and hardly breathed as he listened.

'This is far enough,' said a voice, which was evidently that of the gentleman. 'I will not allow the young lady to go any farther. Now, for what purpose have you brought us to this strange, dark place?'

'I told you before,' replied Nancy, 'that I was afraid to speak to you there. I don't know why it is, but I am so frightened tonight that I can hardly stand.'

'Frightened of what?' asked the gentleman, who seemed to pity her.

'I hardly know of what,' replied the girl. 'I wish I did. Horrible thoughts of death and blood have been in my mind all day.'

'You were not here last Sunday night,' said the gentleman.

'I couldn't come,' replied Nancy. 'I was kept by force.'

'By whom?'

'Him that I told the young lady of before.'

'You were not suspected of holding any communication with anybody on the subject which has brought us here tonight, I hope?' asked the old gentleman.

'No,' replied the girl, shaking her head.

'Good,' said the gentleman. 'Now listen to me. This young lady has communicated to me, and to some other friends who can be safely trusted, what you told her nearly a fortnight ago. I feel I can trust you, and therefore I shall tell you without reserve that we are determined to force the secret, whatever it is, from this man Monks. Put Monks into my hands, and leave him to me to deal with.'

'What if he turns against Fagin and the others?'

'I promise you that in that case, if the truth is forced from him, there the matter will rest; the others shall go free.'

'And if it is not?' asked the girl.

'Then,' said the gentleman, 'this Fagin shall not be brought to justice without your consent.'

'Have I the lady's promise for that?' asked the girl.

'You have,' replied Rose. 'My true and faithful promise.'

'Monks would never learn how you knew what you know?' said the girl after a short pause.

'Never,' replied the gentleman.

'I have lied, and been with others who lie, since I was a little child,' said the girl, after another pause, 'but I will believe you.'

Then, in a very low voice, she started to describe the public house where Monks was to be found, and the night and hour on which Monks usually visited. 'He is tall,' said the girl, 'and a strongly built man; and as he walks, he constantly looks over his shoulder — first on one side, and then on the other. His eyes are deeply sunk in his head, and his face is dark like his hair and eyes. I think that's all I can tell you about him. Wait, though,' she added. 'On his throat there is —'

'A broad red mark, like a burn?' cried the gentleman.

'How's this?' said the girl. 'You know him!'

The young lady gave a cry of surprise, and for a few moments they were so still that the listener could clearly hear them breathe.

'I *think* I do,' said the gentleman, breaking the silence. 'Many people are extraordinarily like each other. It may not be the same man. And now, young woman, you have given us most valuable assistance, and I wish to reward you for it. What can I do for you?'

'Nothing,' replied Nancy.

'You must tell me,' said the old gentleman, very kindly.

'Nothing, sir,' replied the girl, crying. 'You can do nothing to help me. I am past all hope, indeed.'

'It is true that the past has been wasted, but you may hope for the future. I do not say that it is in our power to offer you peace of heart and mind, for that must come as you seek it. But we can send you to a quiet place of shelter, either in England or, if you are afraid to remain here, in some foreign country. Before the sun rises you shall be placed as entirely beyond the reach of your former companions as if you were to disappear from the earth. Come! I do not want you to go back to exchange one word with such companions. Leave them, while you have the chance.'

'I can't, sir,' said the girl, after a short struggle. 'I am chained to my old life. I hate it with all my heart now, but I cannot leave it. I must have gone too far to turn back. I must go home.'

'Home!' repeated the young lady.

'Home, lady,' answered the girl. 'Let us part. I shall be watched or seen. Go! Go! If I have done you any service, all that I ask is that you leave me and let me go my way alone.'

'It is useless,' said the gentleman. 'We are putting her in danger, perhaps, by staying here.'

The two figures of the young lady and her companion soon afterwards appeared on the bridge. The old gentleman pulled her arm through his and led her away. As they disappeared, the girl sank down upon one of the stairs and cried with bitter tears.

After a time she stood up and with unsteady steps climbed back to the road. The amazed observer remained motionless for some minutes afterwards and, having made certain that he was alone again, emerged from his hiding place and, reaching the top, ran towards Fagin's house as fast as his legs could carry him.

Chapter 25   Consequences

It was nearly two hours before sunrise, and Fagin sat in his old home, with a face so pale and eyes so red that he looked more dead than alive.

Stretched out on the floor, fast asleep, lay the young man who had followed Nancy and heard her secret conversation below London Bridge. Towards him the old man sometimes directed his eyes for a moment, and then brought them back. He was deeply occupied with his evil thoughts. His plan of discovering Nancy's new lover had failed; for she had none. He was full of hatred for her, because she dared to do business with strangers, and he did not believe her assurance that she would not give him up. He was full of a deadly fear of being discovered.

He sat still for quite a long time until at last his quick ear seemed to be attracted by a footstep in the street. The bell rang gently; he hurried to the door and soon returned with Bill Sikes, who carried a small parcel under one arm.

'There!' he said, laying the parcel on the table. 'Take care of that, and do the most you can with it. It's been trouble enough to get.'

Fagin took the parcel and, locking it in the cupboard, sat down again without speaking. But he did not take his eyes off Sikes for a second.

'What is it now?' growled Sikes. 'What are you looking at me like that for? Have you gone mad?'

'No, no,' replied Fagin, 'but I've got something to tell you that won't please you.'

'What is it?' said the robber. 'Speak, will you! Or if you don't, it will be for lack of breath. Open your mouth and say what you've got to say in plain words. Out with it, you old dog, out with it!'

Fagin made no answer but, bending over the sleeper, pulled him into a sitting position.

'Tell me that again – once again, just for him to hear,' said the old man, pointing to Sikes as he spoke.

'Tell you what?' asked the boy sleepily.

'That about – Nancy,' said Fagin, holding Sikes by the wrist, as if to prevent his leaving the house before he had heard enough. 'You followed her?'

'Yes.'

'To London Bridge?'

'Yes.'

'Where she met two people?'

'So she did.'

'A gentleman and a lady that she had gone to see before, who asked her to give up all her friends, and Monks first, which she did, and to tell her about the place where we met, which she did. She told it all, every word, did she not?' cried Fagin, half mad with anger.

'That's right,' replied the boy. 'That's just what it was!'

'What did they say about last Sunday?'

'They asked her,' said the boy, 'why she didn't come last Sunday, as she promised. She said she couldn't.'

'Why – why? Tell him that.'

'Because Bill forced her to stay at home,' replied the boy.

'Hell's fire!' cried Sikes, breaking free from Fagin's hold. 'Let me go!'

Pushing the Jew away from him, he rushed from the room and ran up the stairs.

'Bill, Bill,' cried Fagin, hurrying after him. 'A word. Only a word.'

'Let me out,' said Sikes. 'Don't speak to me; it's not safe. Let me out!'

'Listen to me,' said Fagin, laying his hand on the lock. 'You won't be – too – violent, Bill? Be clever, Bill, and not a fool.'

Sikes did not reply but, pulling open the door, rushed into the silent streets.

Without a pause, or a moment's consideration, and looking straight ahead of him with single-minded determination, the robber rushed directly to his home. Opening the door softly he stepped lightly up the stairs and, entering his own room, double-locked the door and pushed a heavy table against it.

The girl was lying half dressed upon the bed. He had woken her from her sleep, for she raised herself with a hurried and frightened look.

'Get up!' said the man.

'It *is* you, Bill!' said the girl, with an expression of pleasure at his return.

'It is,' was the reply. 'Get up.'

There was a candle burning, but the man pulled it from the candlestick and threw it into the fire. Seeing the faint light of early day outside, the girl rose to open the curtain.

'Let it be,' said Sikes. 'There's enough light for what I've got to do.'

'Bill,' said the girl, in the low voice of alarm, 'why are you looking like this at me?'

The robber stood staring at her for a few seconds, breathing quickly; then, seizing her by the hand and throat, he dragged her into the middle of the room and placed his heavy hand over her mouth.

'Bill, Bill!' cried the girl, struggling with the strength of deadly fear. 'I won't shout. Hear me – speak to me – tell me what I have done!'

'You know, you she-devil!' replied the robber. 'You were watched tonight; every word you said was heard.'

'Then spare my life for the love of heaven, as I spared yours,' said the girl, throwing her arms around him. 'Bill, dear Bill, you cannot have the heart to kill me. Oh! Think of all I have given up, only tonight, for you. You *shall* have time to think and save yourself from this crime. Bill, for dear God's sake, for your own, for mine, stop before you take my blood. I have been true to you, on my soul I have!'

Sikes freed one arm and took out his pistol. Even in his anger he realized that it would be dangerous to fire it. Twice he beat, with all his strength, the upturned face that almost touched his own.

She fell, nearly blinded with the blood that rained down from a deep cut in her forehead. But, raising herself with difficulty on her knees, she breathed one prayer for forgiveness to her Maker.

It was a terrible sight to see. The murderer stepped backwards to the wall and, covering his eyes with his hand, seized a heavy stick and struck her down.

Chapter 26   The Flight of Bill Sikes

Of all the terrible crimes that had been committed in London since nightfall, that was the worst. The sun that brings back, not light alone but new life and hope to man, burst on the crowded city and lit up the room where the murdered woman lay. Sikes tried to shut the light out, but it continued to stream in. If the sight was a terrible one in the dull morning, how much worse it was now, in all that brilliant light!

He had not moved; he had been afraid. There had been a low cry of pain and a motion of the hand; and with terror added to anger, he had struck and struck again. Once he threw a cloth over it, but it was worse to imagine the eyes moving towards him than to see them fixed on the ceiling.

He struck a light, lit a fire and threw the heavy stick into it. He washed himself, and rubbed his clothes; there were spots that he could not remove, but he cut the pieces out and burnt them. How those stains were scattered about the room! Even the feet of the dog were bloody.

All this time he had never once turned his back on the body; no, not for a moment. Having completed his preparations and cleaned the dog's feet, he moved backwards towards the door, dragging the dog with him, in case he dirtied his feet again and carried new evidence of the crime out into the streets. He shut the door softly, locked it and left the house.

He crossed the street and looked up at the window to be sure that nothing was visible from the outside. There was the curtain still drawn, which she would have opened to admit the light she never saw again. Behind it lay her body. He whistled to the dog, and walked rapidly away.

It was nine o'clock at night when the man, quite tired out, and the dog, walking lamely from the unusual exercise, turned down a hill, along a little village street and into a small public house. There was a fire burning, and some villagers were drinking in front of it. They made room for the stranger, but he sat down in the farthest corner and ate and drank alone, or rather with his dog, to whom he threw a bit of food from time to time.

The conversation of the men concerned the neighbouring land and farmers. There was nothing to attract attention or cause alarm in this. The murderer, after paying his bill, had almost fallen asleep when he was half woken by the noisy entrance of a newcomer.

This was a pedlar who travelled around the country on foot to sell bits and pieces which he carried in a box hanging on his back. Having eaten his supper, he opened his box, hoping to find some buyers.

'And what is that stuff? Good to eat, Harry?' asked a countryman, pointing to some small packages in a corner.

'This,' said the fellow, producing one, 'is a magical composition for removing all sorts of stains, dirt or spots from all sorts of stuff – silk, woollen or cotton. Wine stains, fruit stains, beer stains, water stains, paint stains, any stains, all come out with one rub of this magical composition. One penny a square. With all these virtues, one penny a square!'

There were two buyers immediately, and more of the listeners were clearly thinking about it. The pedlar, observing this, continued to talk.

'It's all bought up as fast as it can be made,' said the fellow. 'There are fourteen factories always working on it, and they can't make it fast enough. One penny a square! Wine stains, fruit stains, beer stains, water stains, paint stains, mud stains, bloodstains! Here is a stain on the hat of a gentleman present that I'll remove before he can order me a pint of beer.'

'Hah!' cried Sikes, jumping up. 'Give that back!'

'I'll remove it, sir,' replied the man, 'before you can come across the room to get it. Gentlemen all, observe the dark stain on this gentleman's hat. Whether it is a wine stain, fruit stain, beer stain, water stain, paint stain or bloodstain –'

The man got no further for Sikes, swearing violently, knocked over the table, seized the hat from him, and burst out of the building.

The murderer, finding that he was not followed and that they most probably considered him some drunken, ill-tempered fellow, turned back towards the village. As he walked up the street, he recognized the mail coach from London standing at the little post office. He almost knew what was to come, but he crossed over and listened.

The post master came out with the letter bag, which he handed to the guard.

'Anything new in town?' he asked.

'No, nothing that I know of,' the guard replied. 'The price of corn is up a little. I heard talk of a murder, too.'

'That's quite true,' said a gentleman inside the coach, who was looking out of the window. 'And a terrible murder it was.'

'Was it, sir?' said the guard. 'Man or woman?'

'A woman,' replied the gentleman. 'They say –'

Sikes did not wait to hear any more. He took the road leading out of the village and, as he walked into the darkness of the road, he felt a great fear coming over him. Every object in front of him took on the shape of some fearful thing. But these fears were nothing compared to the thought of the girl's murdered body following at his heels. He could sense its shadow, and note how stiffly it seemed to move. He could hear the movement of its clothes, and every breath of wind carried to him that last low cry. If he stopped, it did the same. If he ran, it followed.

At times he turned, with a desperate determination to beat this shadow off. But the hair rose on his head, and his blood stood still, for it had turned with him and was behind him then. He had kept it in front of him that morning, but it was behind him now – always. He leaned his back against a wall, and felt that it stood above him. He threw himself down on the road. At his head it stood, silent and still.

Let no man talk of murderers escaping justice. There were twenty violent deaths in each minute of his fear.

He came to a hut in a field that offered shelter for the night; he could not walk on till daylight came again. He went in and lay down close to the wall – to suffer once again.

For now a vision came before him even more terrible than

that from which he had escaped. Those widely staring eyes, lifeless and glassy, appeared in the darkness. There were only two, but they were everywhere. If he shut out the sight, he remembered the room, with every well-known object in its usual place. The body was in its place too, and its eyes were as he saw them when he left. He got up and rushed out into the field. The figure was behind him. He re-entered the hut, and lay down once more. The eyes were there.

And there he remained in terror until morning came again. Suddenly he made the desperate decision to go back to London.

'There's somebody to speak to there, at least,' he thought. 'A good hiding place too. They'll never expect to catch me there, after I escaped to the country. I could remain in hiding there for a week or so, and then force some money out of Fagin and get abroad to France. I'll risk it.'

He acted on this decision without delay and, choosing the most deserted roads, began his journey back to London, deciding to enter it when night had fallen.

What about the dog, though? If any description of him had been made public, it would not be forgotten that the dog was missing and had probably gone with him. This might lead to his arrest as he passed along the streets. He resolved to drown him, and walked on looking around him for a pool; he picked up a heavy stone and tied it into his handkerchief as he went.

The animal looked up into his master's face while he was making these preparations, as if he understood their purpose, and he followed a little further back than usual. When his master came to the edge of a pool and looked round to call him, he stopped.

'Do you hear me call? Come here!' cried Sikes.

The animal obeyed from force of habit; but as Sikes bent to tie the handkerchief to his throat he gave a low growl and moved away.

'Come back!' said the murderer.

The dog did not move. Sikes called him again. The dog advanced, moved away, paused, and then turned and ran away at top speed.

The man whistled again and again, and sat down and waited in the expectation that he would return. But no dog appeared, and eventually he continued his journey.

Chapter 27   Monks and Mr Brownlow Meet At Last

It was getting dark when Mr Brownlow climbed from a coach at his own door and knocked softly. The door being opened, a strong man got out of the coach and stood at one side of the steps while another man, who had been seated on the coachman's seat, got down too and stood on the other side. At a sign from Mr Brownlow, they helped out a third man and, taking him between them, hurried him into the house. This man was Monks.

They walked in the same manner upstairs without speaking, and Mr Brownlow led the way into a back room. At the door of this room Monks stopped. The two men looked to the old gentleman for instructions.

'If he refuses to obey you,' said Mr Brownlow, 'drag him into the street, call the police and let them arrest him as a criminal.'

'How dare you say that of me?' asked Monks.

'How dare you drive me to it, young man?' said Mr Brownlow. 'Are you mad enough to leave this house? Release him. There, sir, you are free to go, and we to follow. But I warn you that the moment you set foot in the street I'll have you arrested.'

'By what authority have I been seized in the street and brought here by these dogs?' asked Monks, looking from one to the other of the men who stood beside him.

'By mine,' replied Mr Brownlow. 'If you complain of losing

your freedom, ask for the protection of the law. I will appeal to the law too. But do not ask me for pity when it is too late.'

Monks was clearly alarmed. He looked unsure about his next move.

'You will decide quickly,' said Mr Brownlow, firmly. 'If you want me to charge you in public, you know the way. If not, and you wish to appeal for my forgiveness and that of those whom you have deeply injured, seat yourself without a word in that chair. It has waited for you for two whole days.'

Monks looked at the old gentleman with an anxious eye; but, reading in his face nothing but a firm determination, he walked into the room and sat down.

'Lock the door on the outside,' said Mr Brownlow to the two men, 'and come when I ring.'

The men obeyed, and the two were left alone together. 'This is pretty treatment, sir,' said Monks, throwing down his hat and coat, 'from my father's oldest friend.'

'It is because I was your father's oldest friend, young man,' returned Mr Brownlow, 'it is because he knelt with me beside the deathbed of his only sister when he was only a boy, on the morning that would have made her my young wife; it is because of all this that I am going to treat you gently now – yes, Edward Leeford, even now.'

'What is the name Leeford to me?' asked Monks.

'Nothing,' replied Mr Brownlow, 'nothing to you. But it was *hers*, and even at this distance of time it brings back to me the excitement which I once felt when I heard it. I am glad you have changed it.'

'This is all very well,' said Monks, 'but what do you want with me?'

'You have a brother,' said Mr Brownlow, 'the whisper of whose name in your ear when I came behind you in the street was enough to make you accompany me here, in wonder and alarm.'

'I have no brother,' replied Monks. 'You know I was an only child. Why do you talk to me of brothers?'

'I know,' said Mr Brownlow, 'that of the unhappy marriage into which family pride forced your unfortunate father, you were the only child. But I also know that their marriage was so disliked by both parties that at last they were separated.'

'Well,' said Monks, 'they were separated, and what of that?'

'When they had been separated for some time,' returned Mr Brownlow, 'your father found new friends. *This*, at least, you knew already.'

'Not I,' replied Monks, turning away his eyes and beating his foot upon the ground, as a man who is determined to deny everything. 'Not I.'

'Your manner assures me that you have never forgotten it,' returned Mr Brownlow. 'I speak of fifteen years ago, when you were not more than eleven years old, and your father only thirty-one. One of these new friends was a retired naval officer whose wife had died and left him a daughter, a beautiful creature of nineteen. Your father fell deeply in love with her, and the result of this guilty love was your brother.'

'Your story is a long one,' observed Monks, moving restlessly in his chair.

'It is a true story of pain and sorrow, young man,' replied Mr Brownlow, 'and such stories usually *are* long; if it were one of joy and happiness, it would be very brief. Fortunately one of your father's rich relations died and left him considerable property. It was necessary that your father should go to Rome, where this rich relation had died. And there your father fell ill; he was followed, the moment the news reached Paris, by your mother, who carried you with her. He died the day after her arrival, leaving no will . . . no *will* . . . so that the whole property fell to her and to you.'

Here Monks, who had been listening with eager interest,

showed signs of a sudden relief, and wiped his hot face and hands.

'Before he went abroad, and as he passed through London on his way,' said Mr Brownlow slowly, without taking his eyes off the other's face, 'he came to me.'

'I never heard of that,' interrupted Monks.

'He came to me, and left with me a picture painted by himself of this poor girl, which he could not take with him. He was worn down by anxiety; talked of causing ruin and dishonour, and told me of his intention to sell his property, settle a part of the money on his wife and you and then leave the country and never see it any more. But even from me he kept the secret fruit of his guilty love. He promised to write and tell me everything, and after that to see me once again. But *that* was the last time. I had no letter, and I never saw him again.

'I went,' said Mr Brownlow, after a short pause, 'to the scene of his unhappy love, resolved to find the poor girl and give her shelter. But the family had left that part of the country a week before. It was by the strong hand of chance that your poor brother was thrown in my way. And when I saved him from a life of crime, I was struck by his strong similarity to this picture I have spoken of. I need not tell you he was taken away before I knew his history.'

'Why not?' asked Monks quickly.

'Because you know it well.'

'I!'

'It is no use denying it,' replied Mr Brownlow. 'I shall show you that I know more than that.'

'You – you – can't prove anything against me,' said Monks.

'We shall see,' answered the old gentleman, with a searching glance. 'I lost the boy, and no efforts of mine could recover him. Your mother being dead, I knew that you alone could solve the mystery if anybody could. I searched for you everywhere in London, where I discovered you were keeping company with the lowest of criminals. I walked the streets day and night, but until two hours ago all my efforts were fruitless and I never saw you for a moment.'

'And now you do see me,' said Monks, rising, 'what then? Do you think you can prove your charges against me by an imagined similarity between a poor child and a badly painted picture? Brother! You don't even know that a child was born; you don't even know that.'

'I *did not*,' replied Mr Brownlow, rising too. 'But during the last fortnight I have learned it all. There was a will, which your mother destroyed, leaving the secret and the gain to you at her own death. It contained a reference to some child likely to be the result of this sad connection. According to the will, the child was to have all his father's property if he grew up to be a worthy man; if, on the other hand, he became a man of low character like yourself, the property was to be equally shared between you two. The child was born and you accidentally met him; you suspected who he was because he looked so like your father. You went to the place of his birth where there were proofs of his origin. Those proofs were destroyed by you and now, in your own words to your partner, "*the only proof of the boy's identity lies at the bottom of the river, and the old woman that received these things from his mother will never leave her coffin.*" Edward Leeford, do you still challenge me?'

'No, no, no!' replied the man, fearfully.

'Every word!' cried the old gentleman. 'Every word that has passed between you and this villain is known to me. Shadows on the wall have caught your whispers and brought them to my ear. Murder has been done, in which you were morally, if not actually, involved.'

'No, no,' interrupted Monks. 'I – I – know nothing of that; I was going to find out the truth of the story when you caught me. I didn't know the reason. I thought it was a common quarrel.'

'It was the revealing of some of your secrets,' said Mr Brownlow, 'that was the cause of the murder. And now will you sign a true statement of the facts and repeat it before witnesses?'

'I will.'

'You must do more than that,' said Mr Brownlow. 'You must repair the injury you have done to the child, and carry out your father's will so far as the boy is concerned. Then you may go where you please.'

While Monks was walking up and down the room, torn by his fears on the one hand and his hatred on the other, the door was hurriedly unlocked, and a gentleman entered the room in great excitement.

'The man will be caught!' he cried. 'He will be caught tonight!'

'The murderer?' asked Mr Brownlow.

'Yes, yes,' replied the other. 'His dog has been seen, and there seems little doubt that his master is hiding there, under cover of darkness. The men who are pursuing him tell me he cannot escape. A reward of a hundred pounds has been announced by the government tonight.'

'What about Fagin? Any news of him?' asked Mr Brownlow.

'He has not yet been found, but they're sure to get him.'

'Have you made up your mind?' asked Brownlow, in a low voice, of Monks.

'Yes,' he replied. 'You – you – will keep my secret?'

'I will, if you sign now a true statement of facts before witnesses and restore to Oliver Twist the money and property you have unlawfully seized from him.'

The statement having been made and signed, Monks was released.

Chapter 28   The End of Sikes

Jacob's Island stands in the Thames, near one of the poorest and dirtiest parts of London. It is surrounded by muddy water six or eight feet deep. The island is deserted; its houses are roofless and empty; the walls are falling down; the windows are windows no more; the chimneys are blackened, but they give out no smoke. The houses have no owners; they are broken open and entered by those who have the courage; and there they live, and there they die. They must have powerful reasons for a secret dwelling place, or be very poor indeed, if they seek shelter on Jacob's Island.

In an upper room of one of these houses three men sat in silence. One of them was Toby Crackit and the others were fellow robbers. They were talking about Fagin, who had been arrested that same afternoon. Suddenly a hurried knocking was heard at the door below.

Toby Crackit went to the window and, shaking all over, drew in his head. There was no need to tell them who it was; his pale face was enough.

'We must let him in,' he said, picking up the candle.

Crackit went down to the door, and returned, followed by a man with the lower part of his face buried in a handkerchief, and another tied over his head under his hat. He pulled them slowly off. White face, sunken eyes, hollow cheeks, beard of three days' growth; it was the very shadow of Sikes.

He pulled up a chair and sat down. Not a word had been exchanged. He looked from one to another in silence. At last he said: 'Tonight's paper says that Fagin is taken. Is it true, or is it a lie?'

'True.'

They were silent again.

'For God's sake!' said Sikes, passing his hand across his

forehead. 'Have you nothing to say to me?'

There was a restless movement among them, but nobody spoke.

Soon there was another knock at the door. Crackit left the room and came back with Charley Bates behind him. Sikes sat opposite the door, so that the moment the boy entered the room he saw him.

'Toby,' said the boy, stepping back as Sikes turned his eyes towards him, 'why didn't you tell me? Let me go into some other room.'

'Charley,' said Sikes, moving towards him. 'Don't you – don't you know me?'

'Don't come near me,' answered the boy, looking, with horror in his eyes, at the murderer's face. 'You devil!'

Sikes's eyes fell gradually to the ground.

'Witness, you three,' said the boy, becoming more and more excited as he spoke. 'I'm not afraid of him. If they come here after him, I'll give him up; I will. He may kill me for it if he likes, or if he dares, but if I'm here I'll give him up. Murder! Help! Down with him!'

Pouring out these cries, the boy threw himself on the strong man, and in the suddenness of his attack brought him to the ground.

The three observers did not interfere, and the boy and the man rolled on the ground together. But the struggle was too unequal to last long. Sikes had him down, and his knee was on his throat, when Crackit pulled him off with a look of alarm and pointed to the window. There were lights shining below, voices in loud and serious conversation, the noise of hurried footsteps crossing the nearest wooden bridge. Then came a loud knocking at the door, and the whisper of a thousand angry voices.

'Help!' screamed the boy. 'He's here. Break down the door!'

'Open the door of some place where I can lock this screaming

107

child,' cried Sikes, running up and down and dragging the boy with him. 'That door. Quick!' He threw him in, bolted it, and turned the key. 'Is the downstairs door locked?'

'Double-locked and chained,' replied Crackit.

'The wood – is it strong?'

'Lined with sheets of metal.'

'And the windows too?'

'Yes, and the windows.'

'Do your worst!' cried the desperate murderer, throwing open the window and facing the crowd. 'I'll cheat you yet!'

There was a shout from the angry crowd. Some called to those who were nearest to set the house on fire; others begged the officers to shoot him dead. Among them all, none showed such anger as a man on horseback who burst through the crowd and cried, 'Twenty pounds to the man who brings a ladder!'

The nearest voices took up the cry, and hundreds repeated it. Some called for ladders, some for heavy hammers, and all moved excitedly backwards and forwards, in the darkness below, like a field of corn moved by an angry wind.

'Give me a rope, a long rope,' cried the murderer, as he came back into the room, 'They're all in front. I may be able to drop into the water at the back, and escape that way. Give me a rope, or I shall do three more murders and kill myself.'

The frightened men pointed to where the ropes were kept. Sikes quickly chose the longest and strongest and hurried up to the roof.

All the windows at the back of the house had been bricked up long ago, except a small one in the room where Charley Bates was locked. And from this window he had never stopped calling on the crowd to guard the back. And thus when the murderer appeared at last by the door in the roof, a loud shout declared the fact to those in front, and they immediately began to pour round, pressing on each other in an unbroken stream.

The murderer climbed onto the roof and looked down over the low wall. But the water had gone out, and in its place was a sea of mud. The crowd had been silent during these few moments, watching his movements and doubtful of his purpose. But as soon as they understood it, and knew it was defeated, they raised a cry of excitement to which all their previous shouting had been whispers.

On pressed the people from the front – on, on, on, in a strong struggling crowd of angry voices, with here and there a lamp to show them in their anger. Each little bridge bent beneath the weight of the crowd on top of it. It seemed as though the whole city had poured its population out to see his end.

Sikes was, by this time, thoroughly frightened by the violence of the crowd. But then he jumped to his feet, determined to make one last effort to save his life by dropping into the mud, even at the risk of drowning in it.

With new strength and energy, he fixed one end of the rope tightly round the chimney. With the other end he made a noose. He could put it round his waist and lower himself down to the ground. Then he could cut the rope and jump the last few feet.

He put the noose over his head, and was about to place it round his body when suddenly he cried: 'The eyes again!' Stepping back as if struck by lightning, he lost his balance and dropped from the roof. The noose was round his neck. He fell for thirty-five feet. Then he stopped. There was a terrible shaking of his whole body, and there he hung, with the knife held tightly in his lifeless hand.

Chapter 29   Fagin's Last Hours

The court was packed with people. The eyes of all were fixed upon one man – Fagin. He stood in the dock, with his head held forward to enable him to catch every word that fell from the judge's lips as he delivered his speech to the jury. At times he turned his eyes sharply on the observers to note the effect of the judge's words on them. At other times he looked towards his lawyer in a silent appeal that he would, even then, say something in his favour. He had hardly moved since the trial began; and now that the judge ceased to speak, he remained in the same attitude of close attention as though he was still listening.

A slight noise in the court brought him back to reality. Looking round, he saw the members of the jury turning together to consider their decision. He looked around him; he could see the people rising above each other to see his face. In not one face could he read the faintest sympathy with himself. Looking back, he saw that the jury had turned towards the judge. He could learn nothing from their faces; they might as well have been of stone. The courtroom fell silent – not a sound could be heard. Then came the single word, 'Guilty!'

The building rang with a tremendous shout, and another, and another. When silence was restored Fagin was asked if he had anything to say about why sentence of death should not be passed upon him. He had withdrawn into his silent attitude; the question was repeated to him twice before he could answer, and then all he could say was that he was an old man – an old man.

They led him out of the courtroom through another room where some prisoners were waiting for their trials, and through a dark passage into the prison.

Here he was searched in case he had some means of killing himself; then he was led to his cell, where he was left alone.

He sat down on a stone bench which served for seat and bed,

and tried to collect his thoughts. After a while he began to remember a few words of what the judge had said. These gradually fell into their proper places, and by degrees suggested more. In a little while he had the whole speech, almost as it was delivered. To be hanged by the neck till he was dead – that was the end. To be hanged by the neck till he was dead.

As it got dark, he began to think of all the men he had known who had died like that, some of them as a result of information given by him to the authorities. He had seen some of them die, and had joked too because they died with prayers on their lips. Some of them might have been in that same cell – sat on that same spot. It was very dark; why didn't they bring a light? He began to beat with his hands on the heavy door. Eventually two men appeared, one carrying a candle which he put into an iron candlestick fixed to the wall, the other dragging in some bedclothes on which to pass the night, for the prisoner was to be left alone no more.

◆

Saturday night. He had only one more night to live. And as he thought of this, the day broke – Sunday.

◆

The criminal was seated on his bed, rocking himself from side to side, with a face more like that of a trapped animal than that of a man. His mind was wandering to his old life, and he talked to himself constantly, apparently unconscious of the presence of his guards: 'Good boy, Charley – well done! Oliver, too, ha! ha! ha! Quite the gentleman now – quite the –'

'Fagin,' said the guard. 'Fagin, Fagin! Here's somebody who wants to speak to you. Now sir,' he said, as Mr Brownlow entered, 'tell him what you want quickly, if you please, for he grows worse as time goes on.'

'You have some papers,' said Mr Brownlow, advancing, 'which were placed in your hands for better security by a man called Monks.'

'It's all a lie,' replied Fagin. 'I haven't any papers.'

'For the love of God,' said Mr Brownlow, 'do not say that now. You know that Sikes is dead; that Monks has told us everything; that there is no hope of any further gain. Where are those papers?'

'The papers,' said Fagin, 'are in a parcel in a hole a little way up the chimney in the front room at the top.'

'Have you nothing else to ask him, sir?' inquired the guard.

'No, thank you,' replied Mr Brownlow.

Chapter 30   Conclusion

The fortunes of those who have figured in this story are nearly closed. The little that remains can be told in a few, simple words.

Mr Brownlow adopted Oliver as his son, and moved with him and old Mrs Bedwin to within a mile of the house of Mrs Maylie and Rose. Thus the only remaining wish of Oliver's warm heart, to be near his friends, was granted.

Monks, still bearing that assumed name, took the share of the money Mr Brownlow allowed him to keep and travelled to a distant part of the New World. Here he quickly wasted his wealth and once more fell into his old life of crime. It did not take long for him to find himself in prison, where he died. In the same manner died the chief remaining members of Fagin's band. But Charley Bates, shocked by Sikes's crime, turned his back on his past life and succeeded at last in becoming a farmer's boy; he is now the most cheerful young labourer in the south of England.

Mr Grimwig and Dr Losberne became very close friends. Mr Brownlow often joked with Grimwig and reminded him of the night on which they sat with the watch between them, waiting for Oliver's return. But Mr Grimwig always insisted that Oliver *did not come back.* At this the two old gentlemen laughed loudly.

Mr and Mrs Bumble lost their positions as masters of the workhouse and were gradually reduced to great poverty. They finally became residents in that very same workhouse of which they had once been masters.

As to Mr Giles and Brittles, they still remain in their old posts. They divide their attentions so equally between the households of the Maylies and Mr Brownlow that to this day the villagers have never been able to discover to which household they properly belong.

ACTIVITIES

Chapters 1–5

Before you read

1 Discuss what you know about the story of *Oliver Twist*. Then read the Introduction to this book. What have you learnt about the novel and its writer that you did not already know?

2 Look at the Word List at the back of the book and check the meaning of unfamiliar words.

    a Which five words describe people who make money legally?

    b Which word describes somebody who makes money illegally?

While you read

3 Circle the correct endings to these sentences. More than one choice may be correct.

    a Oliver's mother is

        young.   married.   attractive.   strong.

    b On his ninth birthday Oliver is

        tall.   pale.   thin.   hungry.

    c Because Oliver asks for more soup, he is

        locked in a room.   beaten daily.

        offered for sale.   not allowed to wash.

    d Mr Gamfield is

        a chimney sweep.   honest and open-hearted.

        in need of money.   ready to take Oliver.

    e Mr Sowerberry is

        an undertaker.   a friend of Mr Bumble.

        married to a kind woman.   Charlotte's father.

    f Oliver attacks Noah Claypole because Noah

        is rude to everyone.   calls him 'Workhouse'.

        pulls his hair.   insults his mother.

    g The Sowerberrys and Mr Bumble think that Oliver is

        mad.   ungrateful.

        starved.   in need of a beating.

After you read

4 Work with another student. Have this conversation.

Student A: You are Mr Bumble. Oliver has run away from Mr Sowerberry, who has complained to the board. Tell the workhouse master what has happened to Oliver since the day he asked for more soup.

Student B: You are the workhouse master. You are amazed that Oliver could be so ungrateful and wicked. Ask questions to get all the details.

5 Answer these questions.

a Why did Oliver, and not one of the other boys, ask for more soup?

b Why does Noah Claypole look down on Oliver and treat him badly?

Chapters 6–9

Before you read

6 Oliver has run away. He decides to go to London, which is seventy miles away. Discuss these questions.

a How can he travel to London?

b How can he eat and sleep on the way?

c What kind of people will he find in the big city?

While you read

7 Are these statements true (T) or false (F)?

a The 'young gentleman' that Oliver meets in Barnet is smartly dressed. .....

b The boy buys food and drink for Oliver. .....

c Jack Dawkins takes Oliver to a house in one of the better areas of London. .....

d The man called Fagin is generally very polite and pleasant to Oliver. .....

e Fagin has a box of valuables hidden under the floor. .....

f After breakfast the boys practise picking pockets. .....

g Oliver steals a handkerchief from a man outside a
bookshop.   .....

h Oliver is taken away by a policeman.   .....

After you read

8 Imagine that you are Mr Brownlow. You have just arrived home
in your carriage with Oliver, who is unconscious. Explain to your
housekeeper what has happened, from the time you arrived at the
bookshop.

9 Who is speaking, and why are these words important to the
story?

a 'I've got to be in London tonight. I know a respectable old
gentleman who lives there.'

b 'He's such a child!'

c 'Stop! Stop! Don't take him away.'

Chapters 10–13

Before you read

10 Oliver has been saved from prison by good luck and is taken to
the house of Mr Brownlow. Discuss these questions.

a What sort of person is Mr Brownlow? What do we already know
about him?

b What will the Artful Dodger and Bates do now?

While you read

11 Write the names of these people.

a Who is the kind old lady who lives in
Mr Brownlow's house?   ....

b Who is Mr Brownlow's strange
friend who always argues?   ....

c Who goes to the magistrate's office to
find out what has happened to Oliver?   ....

d Who moves to another house in case
Oliver tells the police about him?   ....

e Who finds the sight of Oliver in his
new clothes very funny?   ....

f Who keeps the five pounds taken
from Oliver's pocket? ....

g Who stops Fagin beating Oliver
after he tries to escape? ....

h Who is Bill Sikes's partner in the
plans to rob a house in Chertsey? ....

After you read

12 Answer these questions.

    a How do Nancy and Bill capture Oliver?

    b Who protects Oliver from Bill and Fagin, and why?

    c Why do Bill and Toby need Oliver to break into the house in Chertsey?

13 Work with another student. Have this conversation.

    Student A: You are Toby Crackit. You are planning to rob the house in Chertsey. Tell Bill what there is to steal. Tell him that the servants won't help. Ask if he has any ideas.

    Student B: You are Bill Sikes. Ask Toby what he has found out about the house in Chertsey. Tell him your plan.

Chapters 14–17

Before you read

14 Oliver has been shot. Discuss these questions.

    a What will happen to Oliver if Sikes and Crackit run away and leave him?

    b What will happen if they take him back to Fagin?

While you read

15 Circle the right words.

    a The servants from the house *find/do not find* the wounded Oliver.

    b Oliver has been shot in the *arm/leg* by *Mr Giles/Mr Crackit*.

    c The servants find Oliver *in the garden/on the doorstep*.

    d Monks wants Oliver to be *arrested/killed*.

e Monks and Fagin are worried because *Nancy / Mr Brownlow* is showing a fondness for Oliver.

f Dr Losberne examines Oliver *before / after* Mrs Maylie and Rose see the boy.

g Mrs Maylie and Rose are surprised to see that Oliver is so *ill / young*.

h When the police arrive, Mr Giles finally agrees that Oliver was *probably / probably not* one of the burglars.

After you read

16 Who is the speaker, who or what are they talking about, and what do their words tell you about them?

a 'Here's a thief, madam! Wounded, madam! I shot him, madam!'

b 'I saw it was not easy to train him to the business.'

c 'Kill the girl.'

d 'But even if he has behaved badly, think how young he is.'

17 Imagine that you are Mr Giles.

a Tell the cook and the housemaid what happened in the night. (You were the brave hero, of course.)

b Now give the policemen a more accurate account of what happened that night and the next morning.

Chapters 18–21

Before you read

18 Discuss these questions.

a Oliver is now living in the country with kind and loving people. What can go wrong for him now?

b In the next chapters Nancy plays an important part in the story. What do you already know about her?

19 Number these events in the correct order, 1–9.

   a Nancy looks after Bill Sikes when he is very ill. .....

   b Mrs Bumble asks for a lot of money. .....

   c Fagin gives Nancy some money for Bill Sikes. .....

   d Nancy and Rose arrange to meet again on London Bridge. .....

   e Mr Bumble meets Monks in a bar. .....

   f Nancy meets Rose Maylie in a hotel. .....

   g Monks throws a small bag into the river. .....

   h Nancy tells Rose about Monks's secret. .....

   i Monks arranges to meet Mr and Mrs Bumble the next day. .....

After you read

20 How do these people feel about each other? Give your reasons.

   a Nancy and Bill Sikes

   b Rose Maylie and Nancy

21 Discuss what you now know about Monks.

Chapters 22–24

Before you read

22 Discuss these questions.

   a Oliver finds Mr Brownlow's address in London and wants to see him. How do you think Mr Brownlow and Mr Grimwig will feel about meeting Oliver again?

   b Nancy has made promises to help Oliver. What will Bill Sikes and Fagin do if they find out? How might they find out?

23 Complete this summary by writing one word in each space.

Oliver and .... go to visit Mr Brownlow, who is very
.... to see him again.

Jack Dawkins is .... for stealing a silver ....
and appears in court in front of the .... He is not afraid
and often makes the people in the courtroom ....

Nancy tries to go out at .... o'clock to meet Rose
on .... Bridge, but Sikes will not .... her
leave. Fagin decides to have her .... to see where she
.... and who she ....

The .... Sunday, Nancy meets Mr ....
and Rose. She describes .... to them. He has a red
mark on his .... They offer to take Nancy out of
London to a .... place, but she says she cannot be
....

After you read

24 Work in groups of four and take part in Jack Dawkins's trial.

Student A: You are one of the magistrates. Your job is to find
out whether Dawkins is a thief. If so, he must be
punished.

Student B: You are Dawkins in court. You know you are guilty
and you want to impress and entertain the crowd.

Student C: You are the policeman giving evidence against
Dawkins. You saw him steal the snuff-box and it was
in his pocket when you arrested him.

Student D: You are the clerk of the court. Try to keep order.

25 Discuss Nancy's character and life experiences. Can she be
helped, do you think? How/Why not?

Chapters 25–30

Before you read

26 Discuss these questions.

    a Why are Fagin and Sikes so afraid of what Nancy is doing?

    b How do you think the story will end for each of these characters?

    Oliver Monks Fagin Bill Sikes Nancy

While you read

27 Are these statements true (T) or false (F)?

    a Bill goes to his house and shoots Nancy.   .....

    b Bill escapes into the country but then returns to London.   .....

    c Mr Brownlow goes to Monks's house to talk to him.   .....

    d Mr Brownlow was a friend of Monks's father's.   .....

    e Monks's father was also Oliver's father.   .....

    f Bill Sikes kills himself accidentally while trying to escape.   .....

    g Fagin has some papers belonging to Monks.   .....

    h Oliver's story has a happy ending.   .....

    i All Fagin's thieves die in prison except for the Artful Dodger.   .....

    j Monks lives for many years in America.   .....

After you read

28 Work with another student. Have this conversation.

    Student A: You were in the crowd on Jacob's Island, hoping for part of the £100 reward for Bill Sikes's capture. Tell your friend what you saw. Then ask about Fagin's trial.

    Student B: Ask questions about what happened on Jacob's Island. Then tell your friend about Fagin's trial and his hanging. You watched both events.

29 Discuss how, at the end of the story, Oliver is happy and rich.

Writing

30 Describe how Oliver is different in character from the other boys who steal for Fagin.

31 Dickens introduces a few amusing characters into the story to lighten the drama. Write about Mr Grimwig, Mr Giles or the magistrate, Mr Fang, and describe their role in the story.

32 Who are the true villains in the story? To what extent do they get what they deserve?

33 Write a report for a newspaper about Fagin's trial and death. Use your imagination to add detail to your account.

34 Imagine that you are Monks, living in America. You are in prison and in debt. Write a letter to Oliver asking for money and help.

35 What does Dickens teach his readers about conditions in the workhouses and life in London at this time?

36 Write a letter from Oliver to Charley Bates. It is two years after the end of the book and Bates is now an honest farm worker. Tell him about your life now and invite him to visit you in London.

37 Which are the more interesting characters to read about: the good people like Mr Brownlow and Rose Maylie, or the evil villains like Fagin and Sikes? Explain why.

38 Write the story of Oliver's life in London if he had never met Mr Brownlow.

39 Write a book report for someone who is considering reading *Oliver Twist.* Without spoiling the story by telling too much of it, explain why you did or did not enjoy it.

WORD LIST

allowance (n) money that someone is given regularly

apprentice (n) someone who works for an employer for an agreed amount of time to learn a skill

artful (adj) good at deceiving people

bolt (n/v) a metal bar that slides across to lock a door or window

cast (v) to throw; when you **cast a vote**, you vote in an election

coffin (n) the box in which a dead person is buried

conclude (v) to decide something after considering all the information that you have

contempt (n) a feeling that someone or something does not deserve any respect

determination (n) decisiveness

dodge (v) to move suddenly to the side to avoid someone or something

dwelling (n) a house or other building where people live

exposure (n) the state of being in a situation where something affects you

growl (n/v) the deep, angry sound of an animal

maid (n) a female servant

miser (n) someone who hates spending money and likes to have a lot of it

noose (n) a circle of rope that becomes tighter as it is pulled

pedlar (n) someone who used to walk from place to place selling small things

peel (n) the skin of a fruit or vegetable that you remove before eating it

pistol (n) a small gun that you hold in one hand

pocketbook (n) a wallet or a purse

resolution (n) the final solving of a problem

restore (v) to give something back; to cause someone to return to a state that they were in earlier

snuff (n) powdered tobacco which people breathe in through their nose

specimen (n) a single example of something from a larger group

terrify (v) to make someone extremely frightened

tinker (n) someone who used to go from place to place mending pots and other metal objects

undertaker (n) someone whose job is to arrange funerals

villain (n) someone who deliberately breaks the law or harms people

virtue (n) morally good behaviour; a good quality in someone's character

workhouse (n) a place where, in the past, very poor people lived

Great Expectations
Charles Dickens

Pip is a poor orphan whose life is changed for ever by two very different meetings – one with an escaped convict and the other with an eccentric old lady and the beautiful girl who lives with her. And who is the mysterious person who leaves him a fortune?

Crime and Punishment
Fyodor Dostoevsky

Raskolnikoff, a young student, has been forced to give up his university studies because of lack of money. He withdraws from society and, poor and lonely, he develops a plan to murder a greedy old moneylender. Surely the murder of one worthless old woman would be excused, even approved of, if it made possible a thousand good deeds? But this crime is just the beginning of the story. Afterwards he must go on a journey of self-discovery. He must try to understand his motives and explain them to others. Can he succeed?

Les Misérables
Victor Hugo

Jean Valjean is free at last after nineteen years in prison. Cold and hungry, he is rejected by everyone he meets. But Jean's life is changed forever when he discovers love. He spends the rest of his life helping people, like himself, who have been victims of poverty and social injustice – 'les misérables'.

There are hundreds of Penguin Readers to choose from – world classics, film adaptations, modern-day crime and adventure, short stories, biographies, American classics, non-fiction, plays ...

For a complete list of all Penguin Readers titles, please contact your local Pearson Longman office or visit our website.